Entangled

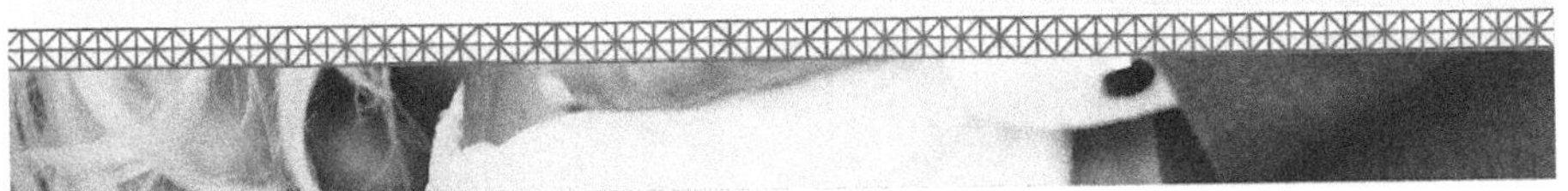

T.M. WELLS

Entangled

By T.M. Wells

COPYRIGHT

Entangled
Written by T.M.Wells
First Edition 2015

Copyright 2015 by T.M.Wells.

Published by Impavid Press
impavidpress@gmail.com

Cover Design by: Impavid Press
Cover Photo: ©EpicStockMedia via Canva.com
Story and Line Editor: Alethea Spiridon

Digital Edition ISBN: 978-0-9948084-0-0
Print Edition ISBN: 978-0-9948084-1-7

Entangled

Cerise's childhood was not easy. She had to grow up quickly and learn how to take care of herself, independently. The unfortunate events in her past, affected her deeply, leaving her guarded and selective on the people she let into her life. Memories of her past haunted her daily life. When suspicious notes surfaced, she had to sacrifice her independence for her safety.

Cerise did not make time for a 'LOVE LIFE'! Avoidance was Cerise's solution, when it came to love. She did not want to get hurt, the way her mother did, when it came to relationships. She preferred to spend time with her friends. Carter was one of them! Would she risk their friendship for romance? Everything seemed so simple, when she was with Carter.

Cerise was an entrepreneur, with ambitious goals. Her career was her life! She accepted a major business 'Contract' to oversee financial investments, between two wealth executives, who were merging their businesses. It was the biggest opportunity of her career. However, with a sexy-cute CEO in the picture, would this 'Merger' cost her more than she bargained for? Was it a disaster from the beginning? Or, was it the best thing that could have happened to her?

She had to face her past, deal with the present, and make decisions that would affect her future.

To my husband,
for your support, encouragement and always believing in me.
Love you xoxo

Chapter One

It was girls' night out at the Midnight House, a local Toronto nightclub. My girlfriends and I, would get together once a month to dance, sing and laugh. I hardly drank alcohol, except for a glass of wine at dinner, occasionally. By the age of thirty-two, you would think I would know my alcohol limit. My friends were at fault for my drunken state. They were responsible for the constant flow of drinks throughout the night.

"Cerise!" Rebecca yelled at me to get my attention across our table. The music was loud and the base from the speakers pulsed through my body. "There's a guy watching you from across the room." She nodded her head to where he was sitting. I turn my head in the same direction and immediately made eye contact with him. He was intense, almost scary. He did not blink or break eye contact with me.

"Why is he staring at me?" I questioned Rebecca with a nervous laugh.

"He's cute! You should go talk to him." Rebecca encouraged.

"I'm not going to go talk to him. The way he's staring at me freaks me out." I said honestly.

"Suit yourself. How are you ever going to meet someone, if you're too afraid to talk to them?"

Here we go again, the lecture has started, I thought.

"Becky, I agree with Cerise. He could turn into a stalker or serial killer. Just because he looks kind of cute, mysterious and really cute…" Sam voiced her opinion.

"You said *cute* twice," Becky interrupted.

"Well, he is!" Sam giggled. "Anyway, cuteness doesn't make him a nice guy."

"I'd let him stalk me." We laughed at Becky's joke.

I glanced over to where he was sitting and found him still staring at me. His lips twitched into a smile before taking a drink from his glass. I quickly turned my attention back to my friends who had ordered another round of shots for us.

"To friendship...Bottoms Up!" Becky held up her shot glass.

We clinked our shot glasses and drank it back. Ugh, it burned on the way down. I put my hand over my mouth as I swallowed, to hide my screwed up face. I did not dare ask what it was. I did not want to know.

My curiosity wanted to look, to see if the mysterious man was still watching me. I tried to be casual when I glanced in his direction. He was no longer sitting at the table. The server was cleaning the table for some other people. *Strange! Was I disappointed or was I relieved?* Sam, Becky, and I jumped out of our seats, to go to the dance floor, when one of our favorite songs started to beat through the speakers. We danced to a few songs before returning to our table. Actually, Becky walked over to the DJ to request a song, Sam walked unsteadily to the bar for another round of drinks, and I wandered off to the bathroom.

I turned the corner to go down the hall and came face-to-face with the mysterious man who was staring at me earlier. He was leaning up against the wall. *Sam was right. He was REALLY cute.* His dark hair was gelled in place and glistened in the dim light. His chiseled jawline was strikingly sexy and his stubble was well groomed. His muscles were visibly showing through his black T-shirt.

"Were you looking for me?" he asked.

"No! Going to the Ladies Room."

"Need any help?"

"No thanks. I think I got this one."

"Call me if you do."

I had to pass him to get to the entrance of the restroom. He did not budge. I did not realized how narrow the hallway was until then. My head was telling me to turn around and go back to Sam and Becky, but my stubborn side was telling me I could protect myself, even in my drunken state, if he tried something.

When I left, he was exactly in the same spot. I tried to pass him by walking sideways. I stumbled on his feet, which were extended into the hallway. He caught me and pulled me in close to his chest. His smell was intoxicating. There was something intriguing about him.

"I knew it…you're falling for me." He was smooth with his quick thinking puns.

"Sorry, excuse me. That was an accident."

"Was it?"

I pushed myself out of his hold. I felt his muscular chest underneath my hands. My cheeks felt hot and flushed. His confidence was frightening. I quickly left, to return to my friends, without saying another word. His eyes studied my unbalanced walk when I left.

When I returned to the table, Kyle and Carter had joined us. Kyle was Samantha's husband and Carter was my best friend. My friends referred to Carter as "eye candy." Carter made my heart skip a beat, every time I saw him. His sexy dirty blond hair, blue eyes, and rock hard body would make anyone's eyes pop and jaws drop, when he walked in the room. There was more to Carter than his great looks. I saw his charming personality, charisma, kind heart, and loyalty to his family and friends.

"Hey, there you are. We were about to go looking for you," Sam partially joked. I gave her a smile only friends could read into. She knew there was something I had to tell her but now was not the best time. Sam grabbed Kyle's arm and brought him to the dance floor.

"Carter, what are you doing here? I thought it was Kyle's turn to drive us home."

"I told Kyle I'd bring you home. It will save him a trip, since everyone lives in the opposite direction," Carter explained. Kyle and Carter had tickets for a concert at the Molson Amphitheater. This was perfect for our arrangements. We arranged for Kyle to bring us home, so we did not have to worry about driving or taking a cab home.

"Awesome! But first you have to dance with me." I took his hand and dragged him to the dance floor. The DJ started to play several back-to-back slow songs. Carter pulled me in tight. I felt so comfortable and safe entangled in his arms.

The bar had closed and everyone was clearing out of the club. Carter took my hand and escorted me outside after we said goodbye to everyone. My small hand fit comfortably in Carter's larger strong hand. We have been friends for a long time. I was so comfortable to be myself around him…there were no secrets.

"Why didn't we date in school?" I asked Carter in a slurred voice, as we walked down the path towards the parking lot.

"You didn't ask, Ma Cerise!" Carter responded in his masculine sexy voice. He rarely called me by my name. It was always *Ma Cerise.*

I do not remember when it started or how, but I loved it when he did. I belonged to him, in friendship. Actually, his pet name for me made people we dated, jealous. They would get insecure and would wonder if there was more going on between us, other than a platonic friendship. Oddly, he did not stop calling me, *Ma Cerise*, to please anyone. It was something he refused to do. He said — if someone did not trust him, then she was not worth his time.

Did he think I was attractive? I wondered. "I know you're a good…Fuck!" Midway through my sentence, I tripped over my long scarf, which was dragging on the ground. It was a good thing Carter had a hold of me; otherwise, I would have been on the ground without my two front teeth. I started to laugh realizing how my words came out before I stumbled. "I mean FRIEND! I know you are a good friend! Actually, I do not know if you are a good fuck. Whom am I kidding? Of course you are! You are gorgeous, funny, respectful and have a body that girls drool over." I rambled on.

"Ditto!" Carter replied. He helped me get stable on my feet, after my stumble. "I better get you home. I'm parked over here." He led the way to his black convertible Porsche Carrera. Carter buckled me into my seat beat and made sure I was comfortable, before going around to the driver's side.

The stars were bright and the moon was full. The warm summer air was refreshing compared to the hot and sweaty dance club. The roof was down and the breeze felt amazing blowing my hair around. I closed my eyes for what seemed like a few minutes. In reality, it was only seconds, before my head started to spin. I did not want to embarrass myself even more than I already had, so I forced my eyes open. I turned and watched Carter while he drove me home. He was flawless. His dirty blonde hair was neatly in place. His face was clean-shaven. His striking blue eyes were so pale in color they were hypnotizing. He was wearing a black button down Ralph Lauren shirt and jeans.

He drove with one hand on the steering wheel and the other on the stick shift. He glanced at the mirrors from time-to-time, and then over at me to make sure I was fine. I could not help think, "You're so sexy!" *Oops,* I said aloud.

"You always say sexual remarks when you're under the influence," Carter reached over and touched my hand gently. "You're looking hot too." He paused, as if searching for his words. "When you dress like that, it is hard to concentrate on anything else."

"Oh! How hard is it?" I giggled.

"Wouldn't you like to know?"

"Well, yes I would!" I reached over and ran my hand up his thigh slowly, giving him time to stop me if he wanted to. Then I touched him. "Holy Shit, you are hard!" *OMG—I touched him.* "And VERY BIG!"

"As I said, when you dress like that, it is hard to concentrate on anything else." We both laughed.

We were only a block away from my condominium. He parked in my parking spot and then helped me out of the car. His hand was around my waist to support me, as we walked to the elevator. It seemed forever for the elevator to arrive. When we stepped into the elevator, he pushed the button and pulled me back into him. I leaned against his chest comfortably, with both of his hands around my waist. He smelled so good. I felt his hard muscular body against mine; including is hard cock, which pushed against my lower back. All I could think about was sex, sex, and sex.

He opened the door to my apartment and brought me to the sofa. "I will be right back." He returned with a bottle of water and Tylenol. "Take these and drink water, it will help you tomorrow." Carter sat down beside me, pulled off my high heels, and rubbed my feet.

"Awe, Paradise." I let out a moan. "Hey, you haven't answered my question. How come you didn't ask me out in school?"

"I wanted to but you made it clear it wasn't an option."

"Well, we aren't kids in high school anymore. Why don't you ask me out now?"

"I ask you out all the time. We go to the movies, dinner, concerts...should I continue?"

"I mean a real date, romantically." I could tell I was making him uncomfortable. I pulled my feet off his legs and inched closer to him. I hiked my black, skintight mini dress up to my hips, to straddle him. I gave him a kiss on his neck and moved slowly up to his ear. I felt his hard cock underneath me, through my panties. I was wet for him. I wanted him. I needed him.

He moaned and then took my face in his hands and kissed me. I unbuttoned his shirt buttons one-by-one, until I saw his perfectly sculpted chest and abs. I ran my hands down his chest to his pant button and zipper and undid them. He unzipped my dress slowly. We studied each other in silence. Carter tossed my dress to the leather chair. I sat on his lap wearing a black strapless bra, with matching thong. Carter grabbed my hips and started grinding his cock into me, through his pants. With one gentle movement, he repositioned me so I was lying down on my leather sofa. His gorgeous muscular body was towering over mine as he studied me. He pulled his jeans and boxer briefs off and tossed them to the floor.

He pushed my thong to the side and gently massaged my opening before entering his fingers. His thumb teased my clit with swift circular movements. Carter watched my reaction and seemed pleased with the way my body responded to his touch. He softly parted my lips, kissed, and licked my clit and my opening. It sent shivers throughout my body. My body was hot and wet for him. He jerked his cock slowly in front of me, showing off his length.

He put the head of his cock in my opening and pushed in with small controlled pumps, never breaking eye contact with me. He glided his whole cock into me with one push. I moaned with pleasure. My body reacted in ways, I did not think was possible. It was clear, Carter knew exactly how to pleasure a women. His look of desire, lust, and hunger set me on fire. The touch of his fingers on my skin made me greedy for more. My senses were overloaded with excitement. When Carter stroked my clit with his thumb, it sent me into an orgasm I have never experienced before. Everything disappeared except for the hot sensation. I closed my eyes and moaned loudly, my body shook and waves of pleasure pulsed through my body.

"God I hope you don't hate me in the morning," Carter whispered. *That would not happen,* I thought!

"Are you on the pill?" he asked.

"I am, but have missed a few days."

He aggressively fucked me, holding my hips, before he pulled out and came on my stomach. He smiled with a satisfied expression.

"God, you are so fucking hot. Why have we waited so long?" Exhausted, Carter fell back onto my sofa. After a few moments of silence, he grabbed some tissues and wiped my stomach. There was an awkward silence between us. This was the first time we had had sex. We teased and flirted with each other for years, but did not pass the grey line, in our friendship.

"How are you feeling?" Carter asked me.

I was not sure if he was referring to my head from drinking too much or emotionally after having great sex for the first time.

"Couldn't be better! It is late. I better get some sleep." I sat up, put my high heel shoes back on, stood up and walked towards the hallway, which lead to my bedroom. Carter watched, my almost naked body, as I walked. I flicked my hair and looked over my shoulder. "You coming with me?"

Carter followed me to my bedroom, grabbing me and hugging me in the doorway, kissing my neck. "Ma Cerise, are you sure you want me to sleep in your room?"

"Yes, I don't want to be alone. Please stay with me."

It felt so good to be in his arms, in my bed. He felt so safe.

Chapter Two

I woke in the morning with a throbbing headache. I thought I had an erotic dream about Carter, but soon realized it was not a dream, when I turned to find him sleeping beside me. *Oh My God, what have we done?* The sheet barely covered him. He shifted his leg, which moved the sheet and exposed his erection. Shyness, excitement and arousal, flooded my head with emotional turmoil.

"Hey beautiful!" Carter reached over and touched the tendrils, which fell around my face.

"Sleep well?" I asked. He smiled–I knew he did. He did not have to answer. I was not sure what to say to my best friend. "Last night was amazing, but I think we need to talk about what happened. Like what happens now? You have a girlfriend." I sat up and put my face in my hands. "I feel like a slut."

"You are definitely not a slut! Last night was incredible. It felt right."

"What about Nicole? How is she going to feel?"

"Nicole and I are not a couple. We had dinner a few times. We haven't even had sex."

"You told me you liked her and enjoyed spending time with her." I started to cry. *How could I let this happen?* I was always in control.

"Ma Cerise, you know I don't do relationships. It's been eight years, since I was even remotely serious about someone." He started to caress my back.

"It doesn't make sense...you didn't make any serious advances before. It was always innocent flirting and teasing between us. Why now?"

"I could not control myself last night, you were so damn sexy in your dress, grinding my cock." He sat up and moved closer. He moved my hair to the side and started to kiss my neck.

I turned sideways to face him. "I don't think it will happen ever again, because your friendship is everything to me," I looked in his eyes sadly.

"That's where you are wrong. I know it will happen again." His devilish smile was so confident. "For the record, you're fucken hot." He kissed my nose, stood up, and walked naked across my room to the bathroom. His cock was fully erect. "I'm going to take a shower. Join me if you dare."

I lay there in my bed thinking about Carter and the events that occurred the night before. I could not stop thinking about how this would affect our friendship. It already felt awkward.

When he came out of my bathroom, he had a huge smile on his face. He sat on the edge of my bed, with a towel around his waist. He looked down at me covered tightly, with my bed sheet. He gave me a kiss on my forehead; "I think I could get use to waking up with you, each morning." He smiled.

"Ten minutes ago you said you 'don't do relationships' now you want to wake up with me each morning. You're so confusing."

He started to tickle me. "Okay, smart ass! Get in the shower and I will make breakfast." He smacked my ass through the sheet and headed to the living room to retrieve his clothes.

As promised, Carter had my breakfast waiting for me on the table with a note:

Ma Cerise,
Sorry to rush out...I have some last minute errands
to do, before the Gala tonight.
See you later
Carter xo
PS....I arranged for Phillip to bring your car home last night.

During breakfast, I read my email and text messages, on my phone. I replied to work related urgent issues, regarding some investments and set up some appointments. I was preparing myself for a major Merger and Acquisition contract, for my clients. I needed this contract to be favorable, to prove my professional abilities to my clients. I needed to 'live, eat and sleep' with this merger for two months. I had an appointment scheduled Monday morning, to meet with both sides of the merger. They were giving me full access to their financial records, to begin my audit and analysis. This was my chance to make a break into the corporate business world. My business had been successful so far, with personal and small business investments. It was my business goal to work with large corporations. It was my chance to achieve my goals. I could not blow it.

My mind kept slipping back to how I felt the night before. I was so confused. The phone rang and startled me. It was Rebecca checking up on me. Rebecca was not shy. She was a people person and met people easily. She was stunning, with curly red hair and green eyes. She left the bar with a person named, Mike, who she met at the dance club. She seemed to really like him. I have not experienced a one-night stand before...*or, was Carter my first?*

"Why don't you ever go home with any of those guys from the club? You know they are into you. You need to get laid, girlfriend! All you do is work." I heard her take a sip of her coffee. "Besides, batteries are expensive." We laughed.

"Why do I need a man, when I live vicariously through you?" I joked. "Besides, this merger is my life. I need it to grow my business to a new level. I have dreams to make come true. A man in my life will only complicate my life. My focus needs to be on my business."

"Believe me, I get it! However, a little fun will not kill your dream. One of these days, you will meet special someone. Hey, speaking of someone special, what are you wearing to Carter's fundraiser Gala, tonight?" Carter founded and hosted the fundraiser gala, for the past five years. The gala raised money for the MC Foundation for Sexually Abused Women and Children.

"I haven't decided. Either my floor length black dress with the scoop back that almost shows my derriere or my red mini dress with the floor length lace overlay. Which one do you think I should wear?" I asked.

"Go with the black dress, it looks gorgeous on you. Who knows, maybe you will meet an eligible bachelor tonight. I have to go, Mike is waking up. See you later at the spa."

Before going to the spa, I needed to stop and visit my mom. It was a tradition, for the last five years on the day of the gala, to visit her.

Before leaving, I sent a text to Carter:

Hey Carter,
Thanks for breakfast.
You are the Best! (In and out of bed!)
See you tonight...Cerise

I hit send, then immediately regretted it. I sounded too forward. After I put on my shoes, I grabbed my keys, purse and headed for the elevator. My phone started vibrating. I smiled knowing it was Carter.

> *Hey Ma Cerise,*
> *You should not send me texts like this. It makes it*
> *VERY HARD to concentrate ...LOL*
> *Feel Free to wear your black dress from last night to the Gala.*

I could not stop smiling. I had to tease him more to satisfy my sense of humor.

> *Ok...black dress it is.... However, tonight I will not be*
> *wearing anything underneath.*
> *Hope to see (all of) you tonight*

Chapter Three

Carter was on my mind, while I drove to go see my mom. I thought about the times Carter had taken care of me. He even handled the little circumstances, like arranging for his assistant to bring my car home from the dance club.

He was the youngest, senior partner at Blake & Powers LLP. His family has been in the business law sector since 1920 and is the leading business law firm, with offices located in Toronto, Vancouver, Montreal, New York, and Chicago. He was destined to become a lawyer at a young age.

We met in high school. Grade Ten. It was about a month into the school year, when our teacher in art class paired us together, to do portraits of each other. Carter still had an interest in art and owned a collection of famous paintings. A couple of times a year, we visited art galleries together. We followed each other to University of Toronto, for bachelor's degree in business for four years, and then he continued his studies in law school for another three years. I started to work for a bank after graduation, as a junior financial analyst and gradually worked my way up to senior financial analyst. I started my own investment consulting business, a few years ago.

Having a man in my life was not a priority, ever since I witnessed my mother abused and controlled by her boyfriend, during their one-year relationship. I was not interested in that lifestyle. I chose to control everything in my life. There were times I wished; I was more like my friend Samantha. She was a stay-at-home mom of two beautiful twin daughters and happily married to her high school sweetheart. Sometimes I wondered if I missed the boat on marriage and children. Every girl wanted the happy-ever-after and to be swept off her feet by her prince charming. However, if it meant being controlled, then I was not going to go down that road.

I parked my car. Tears started to well in my eyes. I took a deep breath and walked along the path, I have gotten to know well. I approached my mom and I began to cry.

"I wish you were here, to hug me," I whispered through my tears. I looked down at her tombstone. I had an emptiness inside which no one has been able to fill. She was a loving, caring, and encouraging mother. I was the most important person, in her life. She left me when her boyfriend murdered her sixteen years ago. I remembered the terrifying evening as if it were yesterday...

Rebecca was sleeping over at my house. It was a Saturday night; we were watching a movie in my room and eating popcorn. Tony and my mom were arguing, which was not anything new. Usually they argued about money, the way my mom dressed, or his drinking. However, that night they were arguing about me. "I want you to leave. You are a pathetic loser. I see the way you look at her. She is sixteen years old. You are never going to ever touch her again. She's my baby." My mom sobbed. "I can handle your control issues and your abuse towards me, but I will not allow Cerise to be abused by you."

"I'll fucken do what I please and with who ever I please, including your precious, CERISE." He threw beer bottle across the room. "Come here, I'll show you."

Rebecca and I were scared and did not know what to do. We heard a struggle in the living room and objects getting broken. My Mom pleaded and choked out the words, "Get Off me!" I could not handle it anymore. I ran downstairs to find Tony on top of my mom, strangling her. It was the most horrifying sight I have ever seen. My Mom's eyes were open staring at me. I tried to push Tony off her but he was too strong. Moments later she was gone, her body stopped fighting, her arms and legs fell to the carpet and her eyes were still open, with tears streaming down the side of her face. "Can't save your precious, Cerise, now.... Bitch!" Everything seemed to be in slow motion. Rebecca grabbed my hand and pulled me to the front door, to escape from the house. Tony ran after us–ten steps behind. I remember flashing lights everywhere, cops running after Tony. Then I blacked out. When I woke up, I was in the hospital. My grandmother was sitting on one side of the bed and Carter was on the other. Rebecca and Samantha stood in the corridor, while a police officer asked Rebecca questions.

I was in my own world talking aloud and clearing the debris away, from the tombstone. I heard footsteps of someone walking towards me. It startled me. I turned quickly to see who it is. It was Carter! I stood up and ran over to him, embraced him with my arms around his neck.

He gave me a tight consoling hug. We stood there hugging each other while I cried. After a few minutes, we let go of each other and he handed me a tissue. Together, we cleaned up the flowers and rearranged the candles. We walked hand-in-hand back to our cars.

"Thank you for coming here today. I really needed a hug."

"I will always be here for you, Cerise." He looked down at me. "Are you going to be okay?"

"Yes, I will be fine. Sometimes I wish she were here to talk to. I really miss her."

"You can talk to me, anytime."

"What if I need to talk to her, about you?"

"Oh I see... Well, you can talk about me, with me, too." He started to smile softly. "Good or bad, doesn't matter."

"Its good, Carter," I smiled at him shyly, and then looked at the pebbles of rocks by our feet. He approached me slowly and kissed me gently on my lips. I melted away. I had forgotten how the butterflies in my stomach made me flustered, heated, and nervous.

"You have to be at the spa by eleven, right?" He asked with our lips still touching and our eyes closed. I nodded yes.

"You have an hour. Do you want to go for a walk on the beach?"

"Sounds romantic." I teased him.

"Honestly, I want to take you back to my apartment right now, but we both know you wouldn't make it back in time for your spa appointment." I smacked his arm playfully.

The beach was five minutes away. He insisted we drive together, in his car, to the beach. Then, he would drive me to the spa, for 11:00. He dialed his assistant's cell number. "Hey Phillip, I have another request. Could you drive Cerise's car to the spa, from the cemetery?" He stopped talking and listened to Phillip's response on the other end. "Yeah she's been drinking again." Carter laughed at his joke, looked at me, and shrugged his shoulders. I smacked Carter's arm again. He ended the call after giving the details of where the spa and cemetery locations were.

"You know he's not going to have a good impression of me! I don't think he wants to be my personal assistant." I tried to pout but started to laugh. "Drinking again?"

"You're so beautiful when you pretend to be mad."

Carter parked the car in the beach parking lot and jumped out quickly, to open my door. I held his hand and tried to get out of the car gracefully. "Thank you, Mr. Blake." Carter smiled and closed the door behind me. He took my purse and locked it in the trunk.

I kicked off my sandals and held them by the straps through my fingers. The warm sand on my feet made me smile and relax. The lake was calm. The waves rolled gently over the sand. The warmth of the sun warmed up my skin. It could not be any better than this. Carter took my hand in his, and we walked in silence. There was tension in the air between us. Usually we were talkative and had so much to say.

"Cerise, I'm going to be bold and say what's on my mind." He caressed my hand with his fingers softly. "I don't regret last night. I can't stop thinking about you, and about us." He stopped and faced me directly. "Let's see where this, whatever this is, takes us." He briefly looked towards the lake, and then made eye contact with me again. "Please trust me. I will not hurt you, physically or emotionally."

"What is this? Is it friends with benefits? I have always felt connected to you and attracted to you... But... If it does not work, I will lose my most valued friend. I'm not sure it's a risk I want to take."

"Will you at least think about it?"

"My life is so busy right now. I have this merger contract right now. You know how important it is to me. I do not think I can do both. This is my opportunity to grow my business."

His expression clearly stated... *'Really? You are brushing me off with that excuse.'*

"Ok! I promise I'll think about it." Carter smiled and gave me a huge hug and lifted me off the ground. My foot instantly kicked back when he lifted me.

We continued to walk, hand in hand. We talked about anything and everything, without any tension between us, as we normally would. We talked about the Gala and how he had to be there early to greet the guests. He regretted he would not be able to escort me personally.

"No problem, I'll meet you there, at 7:00 p.m." I was excited. I truly loved what the MC Foundation had done for so many people. I was proud to support this organization. I regularly donated money and/or my time to Carter's foundation.

"I have arranged for a limo to pick you up, at 6:30." He stopped and looked at me. "I am only excited to see one person tonight... And that's you." He gave me a gentle kiss on my nose. "I should get you to the spa, it's almost 11:00."

Many people, families and couples, had arrived and claimed their spot on the beach, for a day of fun. It had felt like we were the only ones on the beach up until then.

Carter opened my door again, when we arrived at the spa. He stood extremely close to me, "Have a great day getting pampered." I was having a hard time saying good-bye. I did not want our time together to end.

"Thanks Carter, for everything. See you tonight." I wanted to give him a passionate kiss but held back because there were two pairs of eyes burning a hole into the back of my head, from the spa window.

"I'm looking forward to it. Don't forget, you promised, you would think about what we talked about," he reminded me with a devilish smile. "If it helps in my favor, think of how I was naked on your sofa last night." I blushed. It was obvious; we were attracted to each other.

He gave me a quick kiss. "You may have some explaining to do. Sam and Becky have questions written all over their faces. Have Fun."

He returned to his car and gave me a huge smile before driving off. Now I had to face my friends and answer questions.

Chapter Four

"Hello you two, ready to get beautified today?" I asked, as I walked through the front door of the spa.

"You're glowing! Did you take my advice and get laid?" Becky whispered. "With Carter?" She smiled ear to ear. "Cough up the details."

"It's about time, Cerise! What have you been waiting for? He is HOT." Sam grinned.

I started to blush. "Girls, lets get our spa day started."

I loved going to the spa. I tried to make my appointments six weeks apart, for a stress relief massage. Monica has been my massage therapist for the last four years. We have gotten to know each other well, over the years.

"You seem to be a little more relaxed today compared to your last appointment."

"I walked on the beach this morning, maybe that's it." I knew the walk had nothing to do with it.

"That would do it. Physical activity is always a great way to clear your mind. The beach is a great place to do that." She continued to massage my back. "Tonight is the Gala fundraiser. It was in the newspaper today."

"Yeah, we are going. We go each year. It is a foundation dear to my heart."

"Your friend, Carter Blake, is the one who started this fundraiser, right? He is an incredible man for doing this. Organizing this event must take a lot of time to prepare. The newspaper also said, he has done this for the past five years because he wanted to bring awareness to, abuse against women and children, because of a close friend's personal experience. But nobody knows who this mystery person is." I think she hoped I would share any information, since he was my friend. That was a topic, I was not willing to discuss.

"You're right! He is a special person to dedicate so much time to a special cause like this." I started to think about how gentle Carter was. Over the years, he has not exposed my past to anyone, out of respect for me. Because of my history, Carter felt the need to do something about men who were abusive to women and children physically, emotionally, or sexually. In the past five years, he has made an incredible impact by founding the MC Foundation.

I did not speak anymore during my massage. I thought of Carter and about the night, we spent together. Monica left me to relax for a few minutes, before another woman came in to do my facial. She was a quiet individual and did not talk, as much as Monica. I relaxed and enjoyed my facial. I soon joined Sam and Becky, in the next room. We sat in adjacent chairs to have our pedicures and manicures done. Since I decided to wear the black, floor length dress, I requested a French manicure and pedicure.

We laughed about our night out. The funniest moment was when a person on the dance floor tried desperately, to get Samantha's attention. We sat at a table beside the dance floor and this person came over and asked Sam to dance. It was loud in the club, so she politely said no by shaking her head and pointed to her wedding ring. He backed away onto the dance floor. He still encouraged her to go dance with him. The song changed to an upbeat song, he obviously loved. He was excited and jumped on the stage. He danced as the musicians did in the music video. He pumped the air with his hips and mouthed the words of the song. He pointed to Sam and then his crotch. Samantha nearly choked on her drink.

"So Cerise, you still haven't answered our questions. Are you and Carter dating?" Samantha asked.

"Forget about dating, did you see him naked?" Becky asked.

"I'm confused. He's my best friend, and you know how I feel about relationships." I replied, deliberately not answering Becky's question.

"You two would be great together. You have an equal respect for one another." Sam stated and smiled at me.

"Yeah, I agree. You would be the best looking couple on earth." Becky complimented.

"I do flirt with him a lot. I kind of like it, and I think he does too." I admitted.

"I think you should dive in. He really is a great guy, and he always looks out for you." Sam stated. "Last night, for example, he shows up at the club, has a couple of dances with you, and then offers to take you home."

"Not to mention he is the hottest bachelor on the planet." Becky commented.

"What if I can't make a relationship work? Then I lose a friend..."

"Its time, Cerise. He's not that asshole." I knew she was referring to Tony, my mom's boyfriend. "You need to trust your instincts and him," Becky was serious. She was not serious often. She was usually funny and bold with her comments. Tony's name hardly ever came up in conversations. Rebecca knew the reason why I did not let men into my life was due to Tony. There was silence between us. Then she turned back to her humorous self to break the silence. "If you don't take him, I might have to." We started to laugh.

We finished our spa day by 4:30. We were beautified. Massages, hair, nails, and makeup were complete. I drove home with the windows up, to keep my hair styled. I was so thankful for air conditioning. It was a hot and humid day. Once I was home, I made myself a sandwich and checked some emails, to kill some time before putting on my dress. I realized I missed a text from Carter. I had turned off my phone while we were at the spa.

How was your Spa Day?
Did you think about me?
I could not stop thinking of you.
See you soon

It made me smile. I was happy to know, he was thinking of me while we were apart. I responded by texting.

Yes, I was thinking about you too! (As promised)
I cannot wait to see you in your tuxedo.

I did think about him a lot. Another text came through.

I was hoping you would say:
you could not wait to see me OUT of my Tux.

My response:

Flirt

Now I was eager to see him again. I brushed my teeth, touched up my lipstick, sprayed on some perfume, and put on my dress. I stared in the mirror at my reflection. I felt good about the way I looked. My long blond hair was styled into a relaxed twist with curly tendrils around my face. My evening makeup was complete, with dark smoky eyes and a pale colored lipstick. My dress fit snuggly around my curves. My open toed high heels were only visible when I walked. As I looked at myself in the mirror, I thought: *Will Carter like this dress too?*

I took the elevator down to the lobby of my apartment building, to wait for the limo. Through the lobby doors, I could see the limo was already waiting for me. *Punctual*, I thought, and I was early. It was 6:15 p.m. I walked out and the driver greeted me and opened the door of the limo, for me to get in.

Carter was sitting inside waiting for me.

I was surprised to see him. My heart stopped for a second. He was so breathtakingly handsome, in his tuxedo. His sexy smile sent a shiver up my spine. I stepped inside and he immediately gave me a kiss on my cheek. "You look beautiful this evening."

"Thank you. You look handsome as well." I could not keep my eyes off him. He smelled of cologne, which sent my senses wild. "I thought you had to be at the Gala to greet the guests."

"I'm sure they won't miss me," he assured me. "I wanted you to arrive with me, as my date. If you showed up solo, there would be rich bachelors lined up to get your number. Then I would not have a chance."

"There's no one else I would want to be with." I confessed.

"I like the way that sounds," he smiled. "I hope it means you have thought about our conversation, and you too, also want us to be more than friends."

"Yes, it does." I fidgeted with my fingers nervously. Carter smiled and gave me a gentle kiss on my lips.

"I like the way that sounds."

We arrived at the beautiful luxury hotel, in Downtown Toronto. Our driver opened the door for us. Carter stepped out first, and then gave me his hand, to help me get out of the limo. There was a red carpet leading to the entrance. There were photographers taking pictures of the guests, as they arrived. Most guests were wealthy business investors, celebrities, local business associates, friends, and family. There were flashes going off from every direction. One of the photographers yelled, "Mr. Blake, what is your date's name?"

"This is my girlfriend, Miss Cerise Brooks." Carter responded to the reporters.

We continued into the hotel. "Why did they ask what my name was?" I asked curiously.

"Our photo will probably be in the newspaper tomorrow," he answered. "I guess I'm no longer an available bachelor." He laughed. I was surprised he was so eager to let people know, we were dating.

Chapter Five

Carter greeted everyone before entering the Banquet room. The guests all wanted to talk and meet Carter. He was a successful lawyer and seemed to know everyone at the Gala. He remembered everyone's name, which made each guest feel special. I came to each Gala, since it began, but as a guest. I would typically say my hellos, sit at my assigned table, and wait for everyone to arrive before the evening started.

I stood along side of Carter to greet and shake everyone's hands. Carter was kind and included me in his conversations. I could hear people off to the side saying, "Who's the beautiful blond with Mr. Blake?" or "He usually does not bring a date to his Gala, she must be the one!" I became the topic of conversation for the evening. It felt strange to be the center of attention with Carter. Normally, I would watch him from across the room, while he socialized. On the other hand, I also felt comfortable by his side and confident. I noticed Samantha and her husband, Kyle. Behind them were Rebecca and her date, which I assumed was Mike from last night. We welcomed them with hugs and thanked them for coming.

Becky whispered to both of us, "If I didn't know any better, I'd think you two are a couple." She winked at us and walked to her table with Mike.

"Sorry we are a little late, the girls gave us a hard time leaving. They wanted to come see their Auntie Cerise." Sam hugged me cautiously, not to ruin my hair or makeup.

"You'll have to arrange a BBQ pool party, so I can come spend some time with them." I smiled.

"I'm already planning it. See you inside."

There were a couple more guests to greet, and then we sat at our table. I sat with Carter at the head table, along with the gala committee and representatives from the MC Foundation. The banquet room was beautiful. There was white sheer fabric with clear stringed lights, draped over the archways and hung over the tables. The entire room had a romantic, relaxed ambiance. The tables were immaculately set with the best china and crystal. The centerpieces were fresh cut flowers in vases lined with round lemon slices. You could not see the stems of the flowers, only the vibrant yellow of the sectional design of the lemon. The tables had assigned seating with a perfect view of the head table and podium. Each year the Gala kept on getting better. I was admiring the beautiful decorations, when I caught Carter watching me. I would have loved to know what he was thinking at that moment. You knew he was deep in thought, when his facial expression was serious. He was a person who would think before he spoke. I smiled at him. "This is such a special night. The decorations, this year, are incredible. I'm impressed."

"I was thinking the same thing." He smiled gently at me and whispered in my ear. "You're the most beautiful woman in the room."

I smiled at him shyly. "Thank you."

A woman, who needed to speak to Carter, interrupted us. I recognized her but could not remember her name. She was on the committee for the MC Foundation. They spoke briefly. Carter then told me, it was time to formally welcome everyone. The caterers were ready to serve dinner. Carter excused himself and walked to the podium.

"Good evening! My name is Carter Blake. Welcome to our 5th Annual Fundraiser Gala for the MC Foundation." Everyone clapped. "Thank you for coming. I am excited about this evening. We have a couple of guest speakers who will amaze you, with their courage, strength, and their will to survive, followed by an awards presentation. We also have a live band, which will encourage us to the dance floor, a little later in the evening. However, first things first, it is time to enjoy a wonderful gourmet dinner, which has been specially prepared for you. Please enjoy the evening." Everyone clapped again as he returned to his seat, beside me.

The evening flew by. The meal was delicious. The guest speakers were brave individuals. They spoke about how the MC Foundation helped their families in need. I was emotional listening to them. They were survivors of their father's mental and physical abuse. A family friend had sexually abused one of the guest speakers, when she was young. I was proud of them for speaking about their situation and happy that the MC Foundation helped them. It made me proud to be a supporter of this charity. When Carter recognized the support staff, social workers, and the individuals who invested their time to help others, tears welled in my eyes. I would not have been able to speak without crying at that point. He explained, the MC Foundation was successful because of these people and how much they care. He was truly a kind man who did not take people for granted. He cared about this organization and everyone felt his passion, when he spoke.

When I was sixteen, I experienced physical and emotional abuse. Carter was always supportive and helped me through many terrible moments in my life.

Carter ended his speech by saying, "As you know, I started this charity to help women and children who were abused because of a dear friend who experienced abuse at a young age. I saw what abuse could do to a family or individual. I wanted to share knowledge and increase awareness, so we can make changes and better choices for our future. Thank you for supporting the MC Foundation. Please enjoy the rest of the evening."

Everyone applauded for the final time. The live band started to play a slow song. Carter returned to the table, and I gave him a hug. "Everything about this evening is magical. You are an incredible man, and I'm so lucky to have you."

"Correction: I'm the lucky one." He kissed me softly. For a moment, the whole room stopped, and I was in my own world.

"Get a room." Becky interrupted us. A little embarrassed, I let go of Carter and straightened my dress.

"Hi, Becky, so what did you think?" I asked.

"It was the best gala. Congratulations Carter, everything was perfect." She gave him a hug. Sam and Kyle joined our gathering. They looked like a sweet couple, holding hands and looking at each other adoringly.

"What an amazing evening! Thank you for inviting us, Carter. We had an amazing time."

"Thank you, Sam. The night is still young, and there is still dancing," Carter told her.

"Actually, we intended to stay, but we received a call from the babysitter. The girls are not feeling well, so we're going to have to leave early."

"Oh no! I hope they feel better soon. Give them a big kiss for me. I will come by soon to see them," I gave Sam and Kyle a hug. "Thanks for coming."

Shortly after Sam and Kyle left, the music changed to upbeat, faster music. The dance floor was full of people. The bar had a line up. People were mingling throughout the whole room. I was amazed at how many celebrities Carter knew, from doing business with them. I even recognized some of my own clients too. I had given business advice for investments, mergers, or acquisitions to many of these people. Even though I had money invested and was financially secure, I would not classify myself in the same category as most of the people at the Gala. I was not an extravagant person. In fact, I was a conservative spender.

Only my grandmother had knowledge of the insurance plan my mother put in place for me, should anything happen to her. My father passed away when I was five, of a sudden heart attack, and it left my mom struggling to make ends meet. My mom was a stay-at-home mother, and my father was the provider for our family. My mom had no work experience or education. The jobs she was hired for, only paid a little over minimum wage. She could hardly afford the rent and food, on her income. Even though she struggled financially, she paid into a term life insurance plan, in case something ever happened her. Who knew her life would end so tragically?

Carter had been busy the entire night socializing with the guests. He always included me in the conversations, and I enjoyed meeting so many new people. Through Carter, people found out about my business and were interested in setting up meetings with me, to discuss some investments. I did not bring any business cards with me; so many people gave me their business cards for me to follow up with them.

The music changed to slow music again. We had not been on the dance floor all night. Carter must have read my mind because he asked, "Would you like to dance?" I nodded yes. He excused us from the group of people we were speaking to and headed to the dance floor. It felt like the whole room stopped and watched us.

"Finally I have a moment alone with you," he whispered in my ear, as we danced. "You look beautiful and elegant in this dress but I can't stop thinking about what's underneath."

I could not help but smile. I assumed people were wondering what Carter was saying to me to make me smile so much.

"Well, I will tell you so you can stop thinking about it and focus on the gala," I paused for a moment, and whispered, "Nothing!"

"That's not helping, it made it harder to concentrate," he whispered.

"Very hard, eh?" I teased. "I think I can help you with your problem."

"I'm sure you can, too," he teased back. "I have a surprise for you."

"What surprise?" I inquired.

"You'll find out soon enough."

We headed back to our table and mingled with the other guests. Carter did not let me out of his sight, until Becky pulled me away to go dance with her. We were having so much fun, until Becky's expression changed. It was as if she seen a ghost. Before I could ask her what was wrong, someone grabbed my hand, spun me around, and pulled me in tight.

"We meet again!" It was the mysterious man from the dance club the previous night. I was in shock. *What was he doing here? Why was he touching me?* "Aren't you happy to see me?"

"Please let me go! I don't even know you!" I did not want to make a scene at the Gala. I began to look around for Becky, in a panic. I did not notice her right away, until I spotted her talking to Carter and pointing in my direction.

"I'm happy to see you here tonight. What a pleasant surprise!" He pulled me in tighter. "I think we will be seeing much more of each other."

"I don't think so! Let me go," I said firmly and tried to push him away.

"I was hoping we could have a drink and get to know each other."

"She asked you to let her go!" I heard Carter's assertive voice behind me.

"Well, look who it is? Carter Blake! Are you here to save the day, in front of these people?"

"If it comes down to that! Let her go, Alec. It will save you from embarrassment." Carter was not impressed. His expression was firm and serious. *Carter knew him. How did they know each other? Why is there so much tension between them?*

Before releasing me, Alec kissed my hand and said, "It was wonderful to see you again! Until we meet again, Ma Cerise!" When he let me go, Carter pulled me in close to him, with his hand securely around my waist. *Nobody calls me 'Ma Cerise' except Carter. How does he know my name?*

"There won't be a next time!" Carter growled. Alec smiled at Carter, walked towards the banquet doors, and left the Gala. I was

34

relieved. *That was intense.* I think I stopped breathing, out of fear.

"What was that about?" I asked Carter. It was obvious it was not the place or time to get into details. It was going to be something to talk about later. Carter's mood had changed. There was an unexplained edge to him now.

"We will discuss this later, but I want you to promise me, you will stay away from him." Carter demanded and looked directly in my eyes, with concern.

"I don't understand."

"Promise me!"

"I promise...but why?"

A couple of Carter's business associates, wanted to talk to him in private. I returned to our table and mingled with the other couples sitting there. When Carter returned, his mood had returned to his humorous self. He gave me a quick kiss and whispered, "No one gets to call you Ma Cerise. You are mine, always and forever." I smiled gently and squeezed his hand.

It was clear, the gala was a success. People were happy and thrilled to be a part of such a unique evening. I was happy for Carter. He had put so much time and effort into making the evening memorable.

"It's time for your surprise," he took my hand in his. "Follow me!"

I could not figure it out. Instead of heading out of the lobby, to the limo, we headed towards the elevators. He brought me to a room located on the top floor. It was a beautiful room. Actually, it was the size of an elegant one-bedroom apartment. There was a table set for two, with Champagne, chocolate covered strawberries, and some delicious looking pastries and cheesecake. There was a beautiful living area with fireplace. The bedroom had a four-post bed with a canopy, a sheer curtain around the bed frame. It had a silky comforter and sheet set. It looked so fluffy and comfortable. The room had soft taupe, beige, and brown shades throughout. It was elegant and luxurious. It had a Jacuzzi bath and glass shower in the over-sized bathroom. Everything about this room was romantic.

"This is my surprise?" I asked.

"Do you like it?" Carter asked.

"Oh yes, this room is beyond beautiful." I answered. "Why the surprise?"

"Last night, was incredible." He walked over to me and swooped me off my feet. "But tonight is even more special. It is our first night together, as a couple," he said.

"I did not know you were such a romantic." I kissed him. "It's a beautiful surprise, thank you."

He let me down on the sofa, in front of the fireplace. He opened the champagne bottle with a 'pop' sound and poured it into the flute champagne glasses. He handed me a glass and sat down beside me.

"A toast! To the Past! Present! Future!"

"Cheers!" I smiled. We both drank our champagne. He leaned over, to give me a kiss. No one was around to interrupt us. I closed my eyes and enjoyed his lips. He pulled away from our kiss and smiled at me. He grabbed a chocolate covered strawberry and fed it to me. It was delicious. Then I did the same for him. He reached for another strawberry to feed me again; I licked it and sucked on the side of the strawberry. I knew he was aroused watching my tongue and lips assault the strawberry. I eventually ate the strawberry. I grabbed a strawberry to feed to him but instead of giving it to him directly, I put it in my mouth to share with him. We shared the strawberry and kissed each other. The flavors of the chocolate covered strawberries mixed with the champagne were divine.

He stood up and took my hand to bring me over to the beautiful bed, in the bedroom. He started to kiss me, and his hands wandered over my body. I undressed him— one button at a time. We peeled off each other's clothes and dropped them on the floor. He lifted me onto the bed. He kissed and sucked on my nipples, ensuring both had equal time. He moved down my body to my belly button. I anticipated his next stop. I was sure, it would be the center of my pleasure zone. I was wrong.

He massaged each leg down to my toes, with his lips. I wanted him so bad. He teased me sexually and did not give in, to my begging moans. He turned me over to my stomach and continued to kiss every inch of me, from my toes upwards. When he reached my pleasure zone, he bypassed it again, even though I pushed my ass in the air and moaned as he massaged me, with his hands. He spread my ass slightly and groaned with need. He had will power to continue his teasing game. I decided I could play the same game too. Once he reached my neck, I took over the teasing. He was lying on his back and I did the same as he did to me. I kissed every inch of his body, working my way down. When I reached the center of his pleasure zone, I tickled the base of his shaft with my tongue and licked his balls, without once touching him with my hands. I loved teasing him sexually. I did not think he would be able to hold on any longer, so I continued down to his toes. Instead of turning him to his stomach, I straddled him. His thick, long, hard cock begged me to touch him. His sexual need intensified with each minute that passed. He liked to tease me but did not like it when I teased him. I moved my hips in a circular motion and rubbed the shaft of his erection. We had been exploring each other's bodies and did not speak much except for moans of pleasure.

Looking down at his gorgeous face and body, I realized, he was the only man I have truly trusted. For the first time, I did not feel vulnerable or feel the need to hide from my feelings. His hands caressed my breasts. His gentle touch sent shivers down to my toes. He sat up to kiss and suck on my nipples. He pressed my breasts together. My breasts were full in his hands. He was a man who liked to have control. I have witnessed his need for control in his professional life and personal life. He definitely liked control in his sexual life, too. Before letting him regain his control, I gently pushed him back down to the mattress and gave him a devilish smile. We kissed. I felt his sexual need, in his kiss before I pulled away. I wanted him inside of me. I held his cock and jerked him slowly. Carter put his hands behind his head, with linked fingers. His muscular chest, abs, and arms were perfectly flexed. I inserted his hard cock, slowly.

"Is this what you've been thinking of, tonight?" I asked.

"Yes, it was! You have no idea how much I've wanted you today." Carter grabbed my hips and pushed his cock deep inside me. I cried out with pleasure. He rolled us over, so he was on top and in control. He pumped his cock into me slowly, then fast and hard. I ran my hands down his chest and arms. I closed my eyes. My orgasm was near. The vision of stars and the wave of pleasurable contractions sent me into another world. My orgasm took over my body. Carter watched me lose control during my orgasm. When I finished, Carter pulled out and came on my stomach. He collapsed beside me and pulled me in close. He kissed my forehead before grabbing the box of tissues and cleaned my stomach, then pulled the covers over us. We lay there embraced in each other's arms and eventually fell asleep.

Chapter Six

I was content to stay in my soft hotel robe, for the day. However, Carter had other plans for us. Carter wanted to take me for a boat ride, which belonged to his friend. It was docked, at the Toronto HarbourFront marina.

"Sounds like fun. I will have to stop by my place to get clothes." I said, smiling. "I don't think my dress will be appropriate." I joked.

"Actually, I had Phillip buy you some casual clothes for boating, yesterday. They are hanging in the closet."

"You think of everything." I walked over to where he was sitting and sat on his lap. "Thank you for this. You have made everything so special." I paused searching for my words. "I don't want you to feel, you have to do everything for me." I smiled at him and then kissed him gently.

"I like spoiling you." His hand started to sneak its way up my robe, to touch my upper thigh. His touch made me instantly open my legs, slightly, so he could slip his hand between them. "Wet, already?" He smiled with his devilish smile, which I have gotten to know so well. "Let's go take a shower."

I followed him into the bathroom. We both dropped our robes to the floor and stepped into the shower together. The shower had dual showerheads, opposite each other. We washed each other's bodies. We were slippery, with soapy bubbles. Carter pinned me against the tiled walls and kissed me, with passion and lust. I felt so small in his arms. He turned me around to face the wall and placed my hands on the tiled wall, for support. His hands were placed on top of mine, standing behind me. His lips kissed my neck and earlobe. Goosebumps covered my body when he whispered in my ear, how much his cock wanted me. His hands slowly left my hands and gently caressed my arms, shoulders, back, and ass. His fingers traveled to my breasts, and down my stomach to my core. I bent over to invite him to put his cock between my legs. He did with one thrust. I moaned with pleasure. He held my hips and pushed deep inside of me, repeatedly. My skin was so sensitive, I felt the hot water roll down my back and down around my curves. Carter reached around and held my breasts in his hands, while he invaded my opening with energetic movements. I stood on my tippy toes and balanced myself against the wall with my hands. Carter pulled his full length out slowly, and then slammed into me without warning, leaving me off balance momentarily. I reached through my legs, caressed his balls. My touch made him lose his focus. He withdrew and came on the shower floor.

"Ma Cerise, you have to take your pill everyday." He kissed my forehead. "Otherwise we will be expecting a baby in nine months."

"Do you have any condoms?" I asked. I figured he would have them. He had women throwing themselves at him all the time. He had always been careful when it came to safe sex.

"I always wear condoms. You are the only person, I haven't worn one with." His muscular body cornered me in the shower. "You're the first woman, I've made love to," His tender lips touched mine. *He used the love word. Am I dreaming? I could not possibly be the first.*

"Besides, I know who you've slept with. And you said he always wore a condom." I had only been with one person before Carter and we always used a condom. I was young and in University. I thought we were in love. We had had sex a handful of times before I found out; he did not love me. "I also know you wouldn't get knocked up deliberately, for my money. You're the only person I trust."

"How do you know I'm not after your money?" I teased.

"Well, you're a successful business woman who is a conservative spender." He smiled. "You're an investor, so I'm sure you have your own investment portfolio worth a bundle," he said seriously.

"You do know me well." I stared deep into his eyes. "Maybe you're after my money!" I teased him and winked at him. He pulled me in close and held me tight.

"I don't need your money, I only need you, with me, always." He kissed me with possession. The shower was still warm around us. "You handle my investments for me, so you know what I'm worth... I'm curious about yours," he said. "You don't have to answer, its private information."

I told him roughly my invested value, which was not anywhere close to his net value. He seemed surprised by the amount. I did not have the lifestyle of a multi-millionaire, so it was understandable people would not assume I was wealthy. "I usually do not discuss my own finances with anyone. I usually talk about everyone else's investments." I told him. "You're my best friend, and it feels good to have someone I trust, to talk to." I cleared my throat. "You should know these details. I don't even have a Will, so I'm sure you can help me with that."

"Cerise, you don't have a Will. We need to take immediate action on getting a Will. Everyone needs a Will." He paused in thought. "Especially with so much invested money and assets."

He grabbed towels, for both of us. We dried off and prepared for our day together. It was amazing how Phillip knew exactly my size and taste in clothes. He bought me a white pleated skort, a blue and white striped, silky tank top, and slip-on canvas loafers. I felt great in these clothes. Carter looked handsome in creamy tan walking shorts, an un-tucked short sleeve dress shirt, and leather boating loafers. Most of the time, he was dressed in suits, but he was equally scrumptious when casually dressed.

It was a beautiful summer day. The sun was glistening off Lake Ontario. The sky was blue with not a cloud in sight. The marina was busy with people coming and going. Other people were enjoying a day on their boat, docked at the marina, having a few drinks and socializing. Carter greeted everyone as we passed them and introduced me to some of his boating friends.

"It was kind, of your friend, to let you use his boat today."

"He's trying to sell it to me. I asked him if I could take it for a ride on the lake. So it's ours for the day, and you can help me decide if I should buy it."

"I don't know anything about boats. I don't think I'll be much help."

We continued walking down the dock. I looked for a little speedboat. The only boat at the end of the dock was a yacht. It was beautiful. The exterior was mainly white with some blue trim. It was forty feet long, and '*Life's Journey*' was painted, on the back.

"Isn't she a beauty?" Carter asked me.

"Yes, she is." I was a little shocked by its beauty and the size of the yacht.

Carter helped me step on to the boat. I was impressed he knew his way around a boat so well. On the main deck of the yacht, there were white cushioned leather seats in a semi circle, the steering wheel was complete with gadgets, and there was a door leading to the interior. We stepped down the stepladder into a beautiful room. We discovered

40

a full seating area with a television, a kitchen, a bathroom, and a bedroom at the front of the boat with a bed and closet space. There was kitchen cupboards, and extra storage space for pillows, blankets, etc. You could live on this boat. I loved it immediately. It slept six people comfortably because the kitchen table converted into a bed and so did the sofas.

"Want a glass of wine before we have lunch?" Carter asked me.

"Yes, please!" I answered. "No words can describe how beautiful this yacht is, Carter."

"I know. It's impressive."

We sat on the deck with our wine. It was relaxing to sit and talk with Carter. He was always so kind and considerate towards me. He was too good to be true. He had everything—an education, an amazing career at thirty-two, wealth, and, to top it off, he was the most handsome man I knew. If he was trying to impress me, he succeeded.

"How do you know so many people in the marina?" I asked.

"Well, my parents have their yacht here, two docks over that way," he explained and nodded in their direction. "My brothers and I spent half of our summers here, ever since I can remember."

"I knew you vacationed in the summer with your family, but I assumed it was to your cottage or traveling elsewhere." I paused. "Why didn't you tell me?"

"When I was a kid I had everything I wanted, including friends." He paused. "I wanted true friendships because of who I was, not because who my parents were or how much money we had." He smiled sympathetically at me. "That's why you and I were friends immediately. You were down-to-earth, fun to be with, and so creative about how to have a good time with little money." He moved closer to me. "You are still the same person today, except you are a little older, wiser, and richer than you were back in high school." He kissed me gently.

"I must have been so boring. Most of the time, I had no money to go to the movies or do anything exciting on spring breaks. You could have gone on a cruises for spring break or to Europe, but you chose to stay home." I tried to understand. "Why?"

"I had more fun with you, hanging out, listening to music, and partying with our friends." He paused and ran his fingers through his hair. "Unless you have someone special to travel with, traveling can be boring."

"The only time I traveled anywhere was the year we graduated from high school." Our friends, Carter and I, flew to Florida for a week. I started to smile about the great memories we had. "That was a lot of fun!"

"Okay, I have to ask a personal question, but you don't have to answer." He held my hand in his and stared into my eyes. "Today you told me how much money you have invested." He looked down at my hands. "Never mind, it's too personal."

"Carter, I don't mind talking about it." I said honestly. "I didn't want people to know I was a millionaire at sixteen. I didn't want people to know I benefited from my mother, being murdered." I paused and looked at him. "In fact, I really hated knowing I was the beneficiary of my mother's life insurance policy. I resented it. It did not mean anything to me. I would have chosen my mother, over money. It was put into a trust fund until I was twenty-five, and then I started to play around with some investments. Some were risky, but the investments paid off over time," I admitted. "I have only used the money three times for personal investments. One was to pay my student loans. The second was to purchase my condo, and the third was to finance the start-up costs for my business."

"I know it was a difficult time in your life. I wish it did not happen to you." He squeezed my hand gently. "I have learned that I don't have to be ashamed of wealth, regardless of how it was earned." He looked deep into my eyes. "It's how you live your life today that matters. It's about what you want out of life and how you can help other people in the process."

"You always make everything seem so simple." I smiled at him and lifted my glass. "Cheers to living life for today." We clinked our wine glass and had a sip.

"Knock, knock." We heard from the dock.

"Dad, nice to see you." They both hugged each other and patted each other's backs.

"Your mom and I thought we'd come by for a quick visit." He looked over his shoulder. "She will be here in a minute. Betty wanted to talk to her about something."

"Dad, you remember Cerise," I stood up to greet him.

"Of course I do. How are you, Cerise? We saw you in the newspaper this morning." He informed.

"I am? I have not seen the newspapers today. I hope it was good news."

"It was. We have been waiting for the two of you to make your relationship official." He gave me a big hug.

"Hello, Carter," his mother called out, as she stepped up on the boat. Carter assisted her, gave her a hug, and kissed her cheek. "Looking as handsome as ever, dear," she complimented.

"Hello, my dear Cerise. How are you?" She walked towards me and gave me a huge hug.

"I'm doing well, Mrs. Blake. How are you?" I asked. "It's been awhile."

"It really has been a long time. We have spent most of the summer here on the lake. We are heading back to the house this week. We are going to have a family lunch next Sunday. We do hope you and Carter will join us."

"That would be wonderful," I answered.

Mr. Blake and Carter started to talk business, while Mrs. Blake and I sat down. She was a wonderful woman. When my mother passed away, she would always send my grandmother a fruit basket with movie tickets and gift cards, especially at Christmas, on birthdays, and any special occasion. She knew times were tough, and tried to make it easier in any way she could. My grandmother said she was an angel sent from heaven, to watch over me.

"How is your business going? Carter says you are doing well," she inquired.

"My business is doing extremely well. I am starting a new contract this week. I am excited to be involved with a Merger of this magnitude. I am hoping this will bring my business to the next level of success. I am currently looking for a new office location to accommodate my growth. I am thinking about hiring an assistant soon, too," I explained.

"Wonderful news. When is your lease up at your current location?" She asked.

"In four months," I answered.

"Isn't that a coincidence?" She turned her attention to her husband. "Excuse me, Richard, when is the office space on the tenth floor becoming available for lease?" she asked.

"If I remember correctly, in four months!" Mr. Blake said.

"Well, Cerise has mentioned, she is interested in looking for a new office location for her business. Her lease is up in four months." She made eye contact with her husband. "It may be an opportunity to have an investment company, located in your office building."

"It would. I will get some more details and send it over to your office tomorrow. I am sure Carter could show you the office space in the next couple of days, if you are interested," Mr. Blake said.

"I'd be happy to." Carter rubbed my back gently and smiled. I did not want to invade Carter's workspace. We had been spending a lot time together. *Would spending time together at the office, be too much?* I was interested in seeing the office space. Their office building was located in a great location, in downtown Toronto. The office building is desirable, for its professional architecture and location. "We were going to make a lunch and go for a cruise around the islands. Would you like to join us?"

"No thank you, Carter," replied Mrs. Blake. "We have plans to meet friends at the yacht club for lunch. Next time, for sure. If you decide to buy this boat, we promise not to invade your privacy, too much. You two have a wonderful day on the lake." She gave Carter and I a hug.

"Hope to see you next Sunday, Cerise." Mr. Blake gave me a fatherly hug before shaking Carter's hand and saying good-bye.

We were alone again. Carter took me in his arms and gave me a soft, long kiss. The two days I spent with Carter, seemed like a dream. I could not remember a time in my life, I felt so happy.

"It felt good to have my parents come visit us." He was smiling ear-to-ear. "They adore you."

"I adore them too. Your parents are wonderful and always have been."

"I adore you too, Ma Cerise," Carter whispered. "Let's take this baby for a ride and we will have lunch on the lake."

"Okay, sounds like fun. Tell me what you need me to do."

"You can sit down, relax, and enjoy the view. I will take care of everything else."

"I'm already enjoying the view. We do not need to go anywhere for that," My eyes wandered up and down his body.

"Talking that way makes it hard to concentrate." He started to smirk.

We cruised around the Toronto Islands, which I thoroughly enjoyed. We stopped on the lake, in the middle of nowhere and decided to have lunch. We had made a simple lunch; sandwiches, fruit, cheese and wine. We ate on deck, and soaked up the sun.

Carter casually sat back against the white leather seats. Even though he was fully dressed, he made my body ache for him. I slid next to him. His eyes changed from relaxed to desire, when our legs touched. He stared into my eyes to read my mood. He knew I was up to something because he wore his devilish smile. I played around with the button and zipper of his shorts. I positioned myself between his legs and knelt down in front of him. I pulled his shorts and boxer briefs down low enough, to allow his erection to spring free. I teased him by licking the shaft of his cock from the base to the top. I jerked him slowly. I placed the head of his cock in my mouth and sucked, kissed, and licked him. His arousal was intoxicating. I wanted to please him. I wanted him to lose control. I needed him to lose control. I have never surrendered to someone's needs, wants, and desires. I thought it was about losing control, but I realized, I was the one with control. With Carter, I wanted to give him everything. I wanted to please him, excite him, and make him happy. I pushed him into my throat; I felt his cock pulsing.

"If you keep going so deep I'm going to come. God you give great blow-jobs."

I sucked a little harder, and then pushed him in deep again. He could not hold back his sexual climax. He moaned and his body tensed as he ejaculated in my mouth. I swallowed. He tilted his head back on the cushion with his eyes closed. "You blew my mind." He smiled and then opened his eyes to look at me.

It was getting late in the afternoon, so we headed back to the marina. We cleaned the yacht and put everything back in its place, before closing it up for the day. The afternoon had been perfect on Lake Ontario. My first experience on a Yacht was incredible.

Carter drove me back to my condominium. I had to get back to feed Lulu, my adorable black cat. Although, she was getting older, she was still playful and set in her ways. She had been alone for the night. I always left hard food and water out for her, but I knew she would be upset with me, since I was not home in the morning, to give her, her soft canned food. She goes crazy for it. Carter walked me up to my apartment. I fed Lulu immediately. She purred and rubbed against my calves in a figure eight pattern. Carter sat on my sofa waiting for me to join him.

"Life changed right here on my sofa a couple of nights ago," I plopped down beside Carter.

"It sure did." He lifted my chin and gave me a kiss. "It's been on my mind, but I have to ask." Carter looked into my eyes searching for the truth. "How do you know Alec?"

"I don't! I did not even know his name until last night. He was at the dance club the other night. Becky noticed him staring at me. It was creepy, actually. When I walked to the bathroom, he was in the hallway. He made a couple of comments, and then I returned to our table. That was when I saw you," I explained.

"What comments?"

"When I turned into the hallway he asked if I was looking for him and offered to help me in the bathroom. I could not be bothered with him. He's arrogant."

"Some people never change," Carter muttered.

"How do you know him?"

"It's a long story," he paused. "I have known him since I was a child. Our parents were friends. He was always jealous of me and copied everything I did. He was competitive and tried to do better than me." Carter glanced at me. "It was childish and immature. He attended law school too, but he specialized in commercial real estate and found success there. He has many commercial office buildings and a hotel franchise with locations in New York, Toronto, Los Angeles, Paris, and who knows where else." Carter was deep in thought. "It doesn't make sense why he'd show up now. I have not seen him since our university days. And to top it off, he's making moves on you."

"He doesn't seem to be trustworthy." I said honestly. "I was shocked when he referred to me as *'Ma Cerise.'*"

"That was deliberate. He wanted to hit a nerve with me. He succeeded." He put his hand on my knee and rubbed it gently. "We weren't always enemies. In fact, we were good friends. We hung out in law school and had the same circle of friends. Over the years I'm sure your name was mentioned in more than one conversation." His lips were hard pressed together to a forced smile. Knowing he spoke of me often, made me smile.

"Well, not to worry. He's in the past." I ran my fingers through his hair at he base of his neck. "I'm sure everything was a coincidence." I could tell Carter was not convinced.

"Trust me! He is bad news. Please keep your distance and stay away from him," he demanded with concern. I felt sorry for Alec. It must have been awful to grow up constantly treated as if he was not good enough.

We had a few minutes of silence. Lulu was crawling over us and purring. She was begging for attention. You would think I was gone for a week instead of a day.

"This weekend has been great! I do not want it to end but I need to go home tonight. My clothes and work files are there. I have a meeting starting at 7 a.m. in the morning." He looked at me seriously. "I don't want to be apart from you, even for one night. Would you want to stay at my place tonight and go to work from there, in the morning? You can pack an overnight bag and come with me."

"Sure, that would be fine. I don't want to be apart from you either," I confessed. "You know it's going to happen though. We both work long hours, so there will be times we will not see each other. Especially now that I'm working on this merger."

"I realize that. We will work everything out as we go." He patted my knee.

Chapter Seven

Everything about Carter's apartment was modern. The design and layout of his furniture, was staged professionally. Most rooms were in black and white, with a splash of color, as the focal point in each room. His bedroom had black stained furniture. The bed was low to the ground and had a fluffy white comforter on it. The stained floors were dark (almost black) throughout his condominium. The bedroom window had black stained wooden blinds, which were a contrast to the white walls. The splash of color was a painting on the wall above the bed. It was an abstract painting with striking blues. There was black and white pillows tossed on the bed, with a few oblong pillows, in the same blues from the painting.

I heard Carter in the shower. It was 5:30 am, on Monday morning. Most days he was in the office by 7:00 a.m. He felt the first hour and a half was the most productive time of the day. His staff worked nine to five, so he always liked to prepare his day and have everything ready and prioritized by importance for his staff. He worked until 7:00 p.m. unless his team was working on a case, which requires late nights, which happened more often than not.

Carter walked out of the bathroom naked, to his walk-in closet. A few minutes later, he reentered the bedroom fully clothed in a grey suit, white dress shirt, and grey tie. He was so handsome; I could not stop staring. He did not realize I was awake and watching him, until he came over to the side of the bed, to kiss my forehead.

We enjoyed a cup of coffee together while eating our breakfast. There were a few weekend newspapers lying on the table, which caught my eye. I pulled one of the newspapers closer to me. *OMG!* My picture was on the front cover, standing next to Carter on the red carpet. There was a full article on the mystery girl, "Sherry Brooks." The article spoke of the gala and its success. It reported how many people were there and which celebrities supported the cause. I was still in shock as I looked at this front page. Usually, I did not like the way I looked in pictures but this one was a good picture of us together.

I pulled another newspaper towards me. Again, we were on the front page. This time the picture was from a different angle. In the picture, Carter was holding my hand as he guided me towards the hotel entrance. The headline was *Mr. Blake no longer a bachelor!* Then the final paper had a current date, with a picture of us leaving the hotel in the morning.

"Cerise, you look a little pale. Are you okay?"

"I'm not sure what I feel," I said honestly. "I feel like my privacy has been invaded." I looked over at Carter. "I did not even see anyone around, when we left the hotel." I paused. "What if someone took pictures of us, on the lake yesterday?" I put my face in my hands and started to cry.

Carter moved his chair closer to mine. "It will be okay, Cerise. It was big news this weekend." He paused and started to stroke my hair. "Unfortunately, I am used to the publicity because of court cases and press releases. The media sometimes blows details out of proportion. Look on the bright side, everything they said about us was correct, and each article was respectful. We will not be in the newspaper everyday unless there are events happening. Trust me." He put his finger under my chin, tilted my chin up, and gently kissed me. "You don't have to worry about pictures of us on the boat. I made sure we were far enough away from shore and other boats." He assured me and kissed me again.

"I do like these pictures." I tried to smile. "But spelling my name wrong, is upsetting," I joked and laughed through my tears. Carter smiled and hugged me. We talked a little while longer before Carter had to leave to go to the office. He had a scheduled dinner meeting. It was a meeting, he had to attend.

I had my first official meeting with my clients regarding the merger at 9:00 am. I had only met with Mr. Walker previously. He was going to introduce me to his merging partner, Mr. Lockwood, his financial managers and staff. I was excited and nervous at the same time. I wanted to make a great first impression.

I decided to wear my short, navy pleated skirt with a matching blazer and a white collared shirt underneath with my navy open toed high heels. I pulled my hair up into a bun and applied my day makeup. I was going for a professional, classy, and smart look.

When I left Carter's building, I instantly scanned the neighborhood for people with cameras. I was being watched...I sensed it. My paranoia was getting the better of me. I tried to ignore it and carry on with my day. I arrived at my clients' office building and waited in the lobby. My stomach was twisting and turning. My palms were sweaty. I was meeting both business partners of the merger. Their approach intrigued me. Both had successful businesses, and had a huge department of financial staff to handle a merger. However, they mutually agreed to hire me, to offer my unbiased professional advice regarding investment analysis. Both partners, had their internal team of financial staff working on this merger, but they also wanted an unbiased body, to help with the process.

I heard my phone start vibrating. There was a text from Carter. I quickly turned off my phone so it would not disrupt my meeting or discussions during the day. I checked my text:

Thinking of you and our
sexual marathon on the weekend...xo

I smiled at his text and felt warm inside. Quickly I responded:

Thinking of you, too!
Wishing it was still the weekend!
Sherry...LOL

I tucked my phone away, when the secretary greeted me, in the lobby. I followed her up to the boardroom, located on the twentieth floor. I entered the boardroom, which was full of chatter until I walked in. The secretary introduced me to a few financial staff members who were already sitting at the long table. Before I had a chance to sit down, Mr. Walker entered the room and greeted me warmly. We had already met a couple of times before, so he was the only person I knew in the room. I could hear someone opening the door behind me. I turned to greet the person coming in. My jaw dropped to the floor with shock. It was Alec. I could not believe my eyes. He smiled at me, knowing very well the reaction I would have. I felt annoyed. My cheeks instantly flushed. I hoped nobody else could see the heat in my cheeks. He had been following me the past weekend, to meet me before our meeting. *Sneaky Snake, I thought*

"Miss Brooks, I'd like you to meet my future partner, Mr. Lockwood." Mr. Walker introduced us. Immediately, Alec extended his hand to shake mine.

"Nice to finally meet you, Miss Brooks." I shook his hand. I wanted so much to turn and walk out the door. However, that would mean walking away from this opportunity. I promised Carter I would stay away from Alec. I did not intend on breaking my promise, but this was my dream opportunity to grow my business. This was everything I had ever wanted. My professionalism and focus would get me through this, without letting it affect my personal life. Carter was the best thing that had happened to me. *Our friendship of seventeen years could work through this. Balancing my business life and personal life, would be a piece of cake,* I thought.

Alec Lockwood was professional during our meeting, which was different from the last two encounters. The boardroom was full of staff, to offer their help in retrieving data and reports, which I requested. Majority of the day, I was with the financial staff. There was little interaction with Mr. Walker or Mr. Lockwood. I was relieved; Alec was not in the boardroom, during the day. I found him to be arrogant, over-confident, and competitive. His presence would have been distracting. He was aware of how his physical appearance affected women. His tall, dark, and handsome image would make any living female's heart race. It was as if he was capable of putting spells on women, with his glare. After spending a day in the building, I had realized, there were only a few women working in the finance department. I met only six women, out of one hundred financial staff.

Before packing up for the day, I checked my phone for messages.

Are you available tomorrow around 8 a.m.?
Mrs. Rosh is a lawyer who specializes in Wills at our firm.
I would like to introduce you to her,
Then once you are finished, I will show you
the office space available and take you to lunch.

Carter was always so efficient. No detail ever left out.

Works for me; I need to be at the office at 12:30.
Talk to you tonight.

I was packing up to leave for the day, around 6:30 p.m. Most of the financial staff had already left. It was an exhausting day, trying to get my head around the multiple commercial properties, remembering everyone's name and setting up my data files. The beautiful boardroom had wall-to-wall windows, luxurious leather chairs strategically placed around a long mahogany table. The boardroom was equipped with the latest technology for presentations. It would be my office for a few months. It was the arrangement we made, due to my office being too small to handle the paperwork involved, with the merger. I had my files organized in piles, on the long boardroom table. I was cleaning up my last file, when I heard footsteps enter the boardroom. Without turning, I knew it was Alec.

"Productive day?" Alec asked.

"Yes, it was. A great first day!" I replied

"It would be better if we ended it with a drink or even dinner."

"No, thank you! Mr. Lockwood, there has to be professional boundaries. Mr. Walker hired me to ensure this merger goes smoothly. I intend to be professional and I expect you to be the same," I requested.

"Correction! Both Mr. Walker and I hired you, to ensure this merger is as smooth as can be. Therefore, I am your boss. Since we are setting ground rules. I expect nothing less than one hundred percent focus on this merger. I do not want your personal life to interfere, in any way. It will probably be the biggest merger in history. Therefore, I expect long hours with late nights. I expect you to be present at client dinners, if requested. Also, one more thing, do not take each comment I say, literally. You are reading into everything incorrectly. I am your boss, not your future lover. If I wanted you as a lover, I would have had you already."

His firmness was shocking. I felt like slapping him in the face, for speaking to me that way. I would not tolerate a man treating me the way my mother was treated. I stood there feeling vulnerable and alone.

"Do we understand each other?"

"Yes," Was all I could say. He won. I thought I was being smart by requesting professional boundaries. Alec managed to turn it around and put me in my place, with my tail between my legs. He was in charge. He was in control, without a doubt. He turned promptly and left. I could not wait to get out of there. I was not sure if I would return the following day.

Chapter Eight

It was 7:45 a.m., when I arrived at Carter's office building. I checked in with security, at the front desk. I informed him, I had a meeting with Mrs. Rosh at 8:00 a.m. The security guard called Mrs. Rosh. "Mrs. Rosh will be down shortly. Please have a seat in the waiting room." I thanked him and had a seat.

I watched the businessmen and women walk through the lobby, in different directions. A woman who walked through the lobby doors caught my eye. Either she looked pissed off or moody, I could not determine which one. She had short black hair. I would say she was in her late twenties and was dressed fashionably. Her sunglasses were on the top of her head and she carried an oversized designer handbag. She approached the security desk. I could not hear their conversation at first, but I could tell she was not happy. She waved her hands in the air and yelled, "I want you to interrupt his meeting. This is important."

"I'm sorry, Miss Lee, he has indicated, you are not welcome here." The security guard said calmly. "If you don't leave now, we will have you escort you out."

Her rant continued until the elevator door opened. She stopped immediately when Carter walked off the elevator. Her demeanor changed. She immediately became calmer and friendly. "Carter, I knew you would meet with me." Her facial expression changed into a large grin, then batted her eyes and began walking towards Carter in a slow exaggerated hip walk. He walked calmly over to her and had a quiet conversation. He nodded to the security guard with a weak smile, which told them he would take care of the situation. She touched his arm in a flirty way. She started to cry and then the yelling began again. "She is nothing compared to me. You're making the wrong choice, Carter."

Carter eyed the security guard and gestured him to come over with his hand. Carter requested the security guard to walk the woman out of the building. Not once did he raise his voice or show anger.

Carter took a deep breath and exhaled. He then scanned the lobby to find me. When he did, he walked over to me and greeted me with a huge smile. He gave me a quick gentle kiss on my lips. "I'm so sorry you had to witness that situation." He guided me with his hand on my lower back, towards the elevator. "Shall we? I will personally bring you to Mrs. Rosh's office."

"Do I want to know what that was about?" I asked.

"Probably not!" He answered. "That was Nicole. She is upset I started to date someone else." He looked at me. "We had a few dates, but she wasn't like this. Her true personality is coming through."

We took the elevator up to Mrs. Rosh's floor. He walked me directly to her office and introduced us. She greeted me kindly. She was a beautiful woman. She looked like she was in her forties, but my guess was she was mid-fifties. She had pictures of her young grandchildren around her desk. She had some homemade crafts and colored pictures posted on the bulletin board.

"I will leave you to do your business," Carter said to both of us. "Do you think I should return in about an hour?" He directed his question to Mrs. Rosh.

"Yes, an hour should be plenty of time for our initial visit," she replied.

We started out talking about her grandchildren and how long she has been a lawyer. She was talkative and friendly. Her down-to-earth personality made me instantly comfortable. Then the conversation turned to me. I was not comfortable discussing financial matter with people. I was usually the one with the questions. We spoke about investments, life insurance policies, assets, and beneficiaries. I needed to decide where I wanted my money to go, should anything happen to me—which was difficult.

If I had a husband or children, it would be an easy decision. She told me to give it some thought. It could be family, friends, or charities. It was some homework for me to do before our next meeting. Our meeting was successful. I was happy Carter set up the appointment for me. We finished talking about my Will and Power of Attorney, when Carter knocked on the door to interrupt. "Am I too early?" he asked.

"No, not at all!" Mrs. Rosh motioned Carter to enter her office. "We had a wonderful meeting. We will be meeting again in a couple of days, to complete the paperwork." She smiled professionally and put her hand out to shake mine. "Miss Brooks, it was a pleasure to meet you." She shook my hand firmly. I left her office, with Carter. He led the way to the elevators.

Carter wanted to show me the office space, for my business. We stepped off the elevator, on the tenth floor. Carter explained there was one other business occupying the floor... an accounting firm. The entrance to their office was to the left. We took a right and approached glass doors. Through the doors, I could see everything had a cherry wood finish. Carter opened the door with a master key and I followed him inside. I loved the ambiance of the office. It had cherry wood floors and furniture throughout.

We walked through a beautiful waiting room, which lead directly to the reception desk. Carter led us around the corner to the boardroom, which was to the left side of the receptionist area. It had a table, which fit eight people comfortably. It was perfect for my meetings. I had visions of my clients and myself in this room, discussing investments. We then walked out of the boardroom and directly across were two rooms: a bathroom and kitchenette with a sink, mini fridge, coffee maker, and cupboards for coffee cups. To the right of the receptionist desk were two more rooms. They both had sliding pocket glass doors. I loved the sliding doors. We opened the first office door. It was the same size as my current office space. The space had a beautiful corner desk, and filing cabinets that lined the opposite wall. It was a functional office and had plenty of space to keep my files in order. Then we entered into the second office. This was double the size of the first office. It had corner window with a perfect view of the busy street below. It had a large desk and wood cabinetry along the entire wall. There was a TV installed on the wall, which faced the desk.

"So this is the office space. Do you like it?" Carter asked.

"I love it. It's incredible," I was impressed and interested but wondered if I could afford it. "What does it lease for? Not sure if it's within my budget."

"We can talk about it later. Do you see yourself working in this space?"

"I do, it's more than I expected but exactly what I need." I continued to look around. "It does not look occupied. Your dad said it was available in four months."

"It is still under a lease for another four months. The previous tenants moved locations to be closer to their home because they have small children in school. They had an opportunity to get an office which is walking distance to their house and felt paying both leases for an overlapped time-frame of 6 months was worth it."

"I would be interested in finding out the leasing details. If it's affordable I will sign the dotted line." I smiled. "What about the furniture? Does it come with the lease?"

"For you? Anything!" Carter turned and walked to the front entrance and locked the glass doors. I thought it was strange he locked us in but when he turned and had his devilish smile on his face. I knew exactly what he was thinking. He took my hand and led me back to the boardroom. "Feels like I haven't seen you for ages." He pulled me closer and kissed my neck.

"It's been about thirty hours."

"Exactly! That's forever," he joked.

"I was exhausted last night," I admitted. "I'm not used to this physical activity." I laughed.

He helped me take off my blazer and then took his off too and placed them on one of the chairs. He lifted me up on the table. I was sitting on the edge facing him. He stood between my legs. He put his hands up my skirt, pulled my underwear off, and put them in his pocket. He slid his hand back up my skirt to explore. I was wet and ready.

He undid his belt, button, and zipper and released his cock. I played with his cock gently. He stood there with his pants around his ankles, his dress shirt fully buttoned, and his tie thrown over his shoulder. He had this planned. He had fantasized about having his way with me on the boardroom table. I lay back onto the table, lifted my legs, and balanced myself against the back of the chairs, with my high heels.

"I want you now," he growled. "I'm going to fuck you hard and fast." He pulled my hips closer to the edge of the table and with one push he was inside of me. I moaned. His strong hands held me in place when his rhythm increased. My body jerked back and forth each time he pounded into me. The boardroom table was sturdy; it did not move. Having sex on the boardroom table was risky, exciting, and arousing at the same time; a first experience, for me. He lifted both my legs so they were straight up and rested against his chest. My high heels pointed to the ceiling. He continued to push deeper into me, with slower thrusts. I felt his cock pulsing inside of me, as he came. With his cock inside of me, he moved my legs to each side. He bent over me to kiss me on the lips. "Lunch hour has a new meaning for me,

56

especially if you relocate your business to this office." He kissed me again.

We heard a knock on the glass doors. We both scrambled to pull ourselves together. We left the boardroom to find Mr. Blake on the other side of the glass doors.

"Perfect timing," Carter mumbled under his breath to me. I smiled.

"Hello Cerise," Mr. Blake greeted me with a smile. "Are you enjoying your personal tour of the office?"

"Yes, I am." I looked over at Carter. He knew I was referring to our physical encounter. "It is such a beautiful office space. I love it. Now we have to talk lease details before I make my decision."

"We can talk details later," Mr. Blake avoided the conversation. Déjà vu! Carter had said the same thing to me when I brought up the lease details moments earlier.

I excused myself to go to the bathroom to clean myself up. I stared into the mirror and did not recognize my reflection. I would not have had sex on a boardroom table, with anybody, before Carter. The girl I saw in the mirror was truly happy. I felt free to live and be happy for the first time in my life. I heard Carter and Mr. Blake talking about something, but I could not make out what it was. I joined Carter and Mr. Blake in the reception area. They were casually leaning on the reception desk, deep in conversation.

"Cerise, we were discussing the lease. We really do not want to charge you anything, for this office. However, we know you would not accept that offer. We are willing to comprise and lease this office to you with the furniture, for thirty per cent of what you are paying for your current lease. It would cover the utilities for this office space." Mr. Blake negotiated.

"That would not be fair. This is a prime location. It is a bigger office and much nicer. You could get three times what I'm paying right now."

"Well, we are not willing to take anymore than that." He looked seriously at me. "You are family to us, and it would mean so much to us, to give you this opportunity." He paused and looked at Carter. "And besides, Carter has not been able to concentrate, knowing you're on the other side of town. It's affecting his work." We laughed.

"Thank you, I really appreciate it. I know I will truly love building my business here in this office." I gave him a hug. "I can't wait to move in."

"You're welcome." He said. "I wanted to discuss the date as well. This office is currently vacant, so if you want you can move in anytime. I would be willing to void and forgive the contract for the previous tenant for you to move in immediately."

"That would be wonderful. September 1 is two weeks away. Can I move in then?" I looked at both Carter and Mr. Blake. "It will give me a chance to notify my clients and pack up my office."

"Welcome to your new office." Mr. Blake shook my hand and Carter hugged me around my waist from behind and kissed my hair. Mr. Blake promised to have the lease agreement drawn up and ready in the next day or two. He had a business meeting to go to though, so he excused himself and left the office.

"Congratulations, Miss Brooks!" Carter smiled. "I think we should celebrate! Lunch?" He paused, looked at his watch. "I have two hours before my next meeting."

"Sounds good, I'm starving. I have to be at my clients' office by 12:30."

We left the office and walked up the street to a beautiful little French Bistro. We sat in a private booth, talked, and drank a glass of red wine. The food, cheese, wine, and bread were the best I ever had. The restaurant was romantic with dim lighting. The decorations were from Paris. It was a wonderful lunch. I wished time stood still, when I was with Carter, but it was faster than ever. Before Carter returned to his office, he walked me to my car and kissed me gently. "Can I see you tonight?" he asked me. "I will be leaving the office at 7:00."

"Probably not, it will be a late night for me. I've been away for the morning, so I'll be working late to make up for lost time." I said sadly and kissed him before getting in my car. "Thank you for lunch."

"I'll pick up dinner and meet you at your place when you are ready. Text me." He was not taking no for an answer. "It doesn't matter how late you'll be. I want to see you."

When I left my clients office the day before, I was not sure I would return. It was a bad way to end the day, especially the first day. I thought about it a lot and decided I would not allow Alec to intimidate me. I would not give him the upper hand and interfere with my career goals. I had had multiple opportunities to tell Carter about Alec during lunch, but I decided I would tell him later. I did not want to ruin our celebration lunch.

I was deep in thought when I heard someone knock on the boardroom door and entered. I lifted my head from reading and made eye contact with Alec. He stood in the doorway and leaned against the doorframe. My heart stopped. *Why did he have to show up?* My afternoon was smooth sailing, without seeing him once. I was nervous to talk to him. Each time I met this man, it was not positive.

"May I come in?" Alec seemed in a good mood.

"Sure, it's your boardroom."

He entered and closed the door behind him. *Stay calm,* I told myself. I felt uncomfortable. I started to think about how I could exit the boardroom quickly, or what excuses I could use to leave. I started to regret my decision to return. My anxiety heightened; sweaty palms, stomach turned, and my heartbeat increased. This was not worth it. He walked around the boardroom table slowly pretending to look at the files. When he reached me, he pulled out a chair beside me and sat down. He sat with his legs wide apart, stretched his arms up over his head, linked his fingers together, and leaned back into his chair.

"Is there something I can help with?" he asked.

"No thank you. I'm fine." I dared not make eye contact with him.

"I'm impressed to see you here today." The corner of his mouth twitched into a faint smile. "It shows a lot of character and professionalism on your part."

"Why wouldn't I? I'm here to complete a job I've been hired to do."

"That's honorable of you." I was not sure if he was giving me a compliment or if he was being sarcastic.

"Listen, I want to apologize for yesterday. I realize I came off a little strong." I remained silent. I looked him in the eyes to see if he was being sincere. I felt he was. "Do you accept my apology? Can we start over?"

"Yes, I accept your apology. Thank you, I appreciate it."

"Hi! I'm Alec Lockwood." He extended his hand to shake mine.

"I'm Cerise Brooks." I smiled. We chatted for about ten minutes or so. It was small talk, but it was a start to getting to know each other a little better. He kept everything business related during our conversation, which I appreciated. I had one goal: Merger Contract. Getting to know him personally was not apart of my goals. However, I did respect, he was making an effort to be kinder, compared to the day before.

"It's eight o'clock you should call it a night. I have plans tonight and am not comfortable leaving you in the office alone."

"I'm wrapping everything up. I will be leaving in ten minutes. You go ahead. Enjoy your evening."

When I approached my car located in the underground parking lot, I could hear tires screeching and a horn honk. I did not like underground parking lots. They were too isolated and the lighting was not the best. I have heard about horror stories of people assaulted or raped in underground garages. I rushed over to my car, pressed the button to get in. I locked my door immediately and fumbled to put my key in the ignition. I started my car and put on my seat belt. That was when I noticed the writing on my front window. Someone wrote BITCH in red lipstick on my windshield. It was backwards to me, but easy enough to figure out, what it said in reverse. My heart started beating harder. Panic and fear took over. My body stiffened and instantly I scanned my surroundings. *Was someone watching me?* I pulled out of the parking spot quickly, making my own screeching tire noise. I wanted to get out of there quickly. There was no way I was getting out of the car, to clean it off my windshield. I called Carter through my Bluetooth. His voicemail cut in.

"Carter, please call me. Someone wrote the word BITCH on my car window." I paused. "I'm sure I'm over-reacting, but I'm a little scared. Why would someone do this? I'm on my way to my place."

When I arrived at my apartment, I hesitated to get out of the car. I stayed there for a few minutes looking around. I convinced myself it was no big deal and started to grab my purse and briefcase from the passenger seat. Someone knocked on my window, which made me jump. My heart began to race and my body stiffened. I turned to see who it was. It was Carter.

"Carter? What are you doing here?" I asked.

"Remember, I told you I'd come to our place with dinner tonight. I have been waiting for you. When I received your message, I came down stairs to get you. Are you okay?"

60

I gave him a hug. "Thank you, Carter. I don't understand who would do this to me."

"That's what we are going to find out." He started to inspect the window. He took a picture of it with his phone. "I called Kyle. He's coming over." He was a police officer who specialized in crime scenes and investigations.

"Do you really think it is necessary? It was probably some kid goofing around," I tried to convince myself.

"Yes, I think it should be looked into. People do weird things. Protecting you from getting hurt is what I'm concerned about."

Kyle's cruiser pulled up behind my car. Kyle and his partner greeted both of us and then started asking the usual questions: Is there anybody you think would do this? Do you have any enemies? Has this happened before? Do you get hate mail? My answer to those questions was, "No, nothing like this has ever happened before." I started to worry by the looks on their face.

"There was a woman I dated, who is not happy that Cerise and I are together. Do you think she might have something to do with this? She came to my office building upset and had to be escorted out by security today," Carter reported.

"We will look into it. It would not be the first time an ex wanted revenge," Kyle jotted down some notes.

"Well, she was not an ex. We had dinner a few times," Carter felt the need to explain.

"We will investigate to see if she had anything to do with this. In the meantime we will see if we can get any finger prints off your car." He paused. "Cerise, if possible I would like you to be extra cautious when traveling by yourself or going into isolated places. Okay?" He patted my arm to assure me everything would be fine.

Carter and I had been friends with Kyle, since high school. In high school, Sam, Kyle, Becky, Carter and I were inseparable. Samantha and Kyle were high school sweethearts. I felt secure, knowing Kyle was looking into this for me.

Carter and I went to my apartment, while they continued with their investigation. Carter had a worried look on his face. He sat down on the sofa and stared at me. I put my bags down at the front door and walked over to him. "Carter, please don't worry about me. It's going to be okay." I ran my fingers through his hair.

"This is my fault. This is happening because of me."

"Carter, we don't know anything yet...it may be nothing." I tried to reassure him, "I'm sure it will not happen again."

"Well, to be on the safe side, I'm going to get some security staff." He pulled my arms down gently, to make me kneel, in front of him. "Just for a little while." He cupped my face with his hands and kissed me gently. "I would not forgive myself if anything ever happened to you," he confessed.

"I'm not a celebrity. I don't need security," I argued.

"Maybe you're right...maybe this is an isolated incident. For my peace of mind, I want you to have security for the next two weeks while you are at your current office." He paused. "Then we can decide if we still need security, thereafter. "

"Okay, still not necessary, but I know I can't win this one. Two weeks, that's it!"

I was in my room, changing into track-pants and a tee shirt, when I heard a knock at the door. Rushing, I pulled my hair up into a messy ponytail and inspected myself in the mirror, briefly. I heard Carter talking to Kyle and his partner from my bedroom. When I entered the room, they stopped talking.

"Hi Kyle, everything ok?" I asked.

"Yes, everything is good. We have everything we need," he paused. "We cleaned up your windshield, so everything is back to normal."

"We will run the prints. At this point, more than likely, it is kids vandalizing property," Kyle's partner explained. *Scott? Was that his name?* Everything had been so hectic; I did not pay attention when introduced.

"Thank you," I shook his hand.

Carter was standing with his hands in his pocket. "Thank you so much for coming so quickly." Carter took his right hand out to shake Scott's hand. When he did, my panties he stashed in his pocket during our boardroom quickie came out with his hand too. They hung from the button of his shirtsleeve, by the lace.

The three men started to roar with laughter. I stood there in shock. *Could the day get any worse?* I gently grabbed my panties from his hands. "Thanks for holding on to them, for me." I gave Carter a look of embarrassment.

62

Kyle and Scott teased Carter about having my panties in his pocket. Carter will not be able to live this one down, ever. It will be the story; the boys will bring up, repeatedly, to tease Carter. Carter had a wonderful sense of humor. He loved to play jokes on his friends and have a good time.

Kyle and Scott had a radio call, so they had to leave. They said they would get back to us if anything turned up.

Carter closed the door pulled me in close. "Putting your panties in my pocket makes you a very bad girl." He kissed my neck and earlobe.

"Let me remind you, it was YOU who took them off and put them in your pocket,"

"Oh yes, how could I forget. Then that makes me a very bad boy."

Chapter Nine

Ray was a built man, in his late forties. He was an attractive man, with dark hair and dark eyes. He was dressed in a navy suit and white shirt but no tie. He stood tall and confident.

"Good morning, Mr. Blake." Ray shook Carter's hand.

"Please come in," Carter said. "I'd like you to meet Miss Cerise Brooks." I reached out my hand to shake his.

"Please call me Ray." He shook my hand firmly. "As discussed with Mr. Blake, I will be accompanying you, everywhere you go. I will do my best to stay out of your way, so you can focus on your business matters."

"Thank you. I have not had anyone watch out for me, in this manner before...but then again I have not been the recipient of hate crimes either," I tried to make light of the situation.

"The first few days will be getting to know each other's schedules and procedures, so please feel free to discuss anything with me." He paused then looked at Carter. "As we discussed, I will let you know of any extra security measures we may need, such as cameras, alarms, etc."

"Thank you," Carter replied. "Cerise is currently working out of two locations. She has her own office space. She will be spending time there, packing it up over the next week, to move to her new office, in my office building. The other location is at her clients' office. They have loaned her their boardroom, during this transition. I'm sure once she's settled into her new office, she will no longer need to go there, as she will have her own space." Carter explained. "The incident happened in her clients' underground parking garage, as I explained last night." Carter was business like and to the point. "Here are my contact numbers, should you need to get ahold of me." He handed him a piece of paper. "I expect to get a couple of updates throughout the day and be notified immediately should something happen or seem out of place."

"In addition, I would prefer to drive my vehicle, as an extra precaution. Do you see a problem with that?"

"No," Carter began, but I interrupted.

"Do you really think it is necessary? Someone wrote on my windshield, they didn't threaten my life," I said defensively.

"Yes, initially I think it would be best," Carter said. I felt he was being too protective and controlling. Controlling relationships scared me. I remembered my mother being a strong independent woman, until she met Tony. She was afraid of him. I could remember the times he hurt her.

If she glanced out the car window, and there was a man standing or walking on the sidewalk, she would get a knee punch with his knuckles and a slap on the back of her head to look down. She had to look down in her lap, and not make eye contact with anybody. I felt so helpless, sitting in the back seat while my mother cried up front, with her head down. After a while, she would not wear skirts or shorts because of the bruises around her knees.

"Carter, I think we should discuss this. I don't like these arrangements."

Carter excused us, before going into my bedroom to talk. He closed the door and turned around. He approached me and took both my hands in his. "Cerise, I know this must feel like your independence and privacy are being invaded. I see these sorts of incidents, in the courts, more than I would like to admit. Most times people cannot afford security personnel and it ends badly. We have money. There is no reason not to be overprotective, for a short period, to ensure you are safe." He paused. "I know you're a little mad at me right now."

"I'm mad you didn't discuss this with me first," I crossed my arms. "If our relationship is going to work, we have to talk about these things first."

"I know. I am sorry. Do you forgive me? How can I make it up to you?" He asked and pulled me into his chest. "How does a weekend away at my family cottage sound? We can go up on Friday night. We can stay Friday and Saturday and return Sunday to go to my Mom and Dad's for lunch." I could barely contain my excitement. *How could I remain angry at this beautiful creature?* He looked at me gently. "Am I forgiven?"

"Okay, you're forgiven." I smiled ear to ear and gave him a huge hug. He kissed me before letting me go. We returned to Ray, who was sitting in the living room. Carter discussed the building security and some other details. I gathered my purse and some personal belongings I needed for my day at both offices.

Carter gave me a quick kiss good-bye. It was already 9:00 a.m. Carter was never late for work, so I assumed it would be a late night at the office.

Ray drove me to my office. Balancing two offices temporarily would be a task. I had decided it would no longer be necessary to go to Alec's office, once I was at my new location. I would have more office space, to work on the merger contract. It would be a relief to not see Alec each day, except for the occasional meeting.

Ray was alert and investigated everything. He studied every detail. If asked, I'm sure he could have told me how many cars were parked in the underground parking lot, along with the colors and makes of each of them. I liked him. During our drive to my office, I learned he had a daughter named, Chelsea. She was nineteen years old and in University. I could tell he missed her. He had worked for celebrities and politicians over the years. It was easy to have a conversation with Ray. However, when focused on inspecting and observing our surroundings, he was quiet.

I managed to pack up my files quickly. The remaining items I had to pack were the pictures on the wall, my office supplies in my desk, and personal belongings. It would not take long to finish.

I arranged to take Sarah to lunch the next day. She was the secretary for several businesses located on my floor, in my office building. We shared the cost of the administration staff and phone lines to lower our expenses. Sarah has been wonderful to me. She was an excellent employee but she was also someone I considered a friend. She was sad to hear the news I was relocating my office, but wished me well. She helped me send out my moving notices to my clients and business associates. It was a huge task and I could not have done it without her.

I arranged for the moving company to come Monday morning, to move my files to my new office. Carter arranged with his father to start the lease one week earlier than originally planned, due to the garage incident. It was going so fast.

It was strange, having Ray watching everything I did in a day. He must have been extremely bored. If he was not helping me move heavy boxes, he was doing rounds to check the building and the underground parking. During those times, I stayed in my office, as per instruction. It was a direct order from Carter. I did not have permission to go out of the office unsupervised.

When we left the building to head over to Alec's office, Ray double-checked that my office was locked, then scanned the parking lot and the surrounding area before getting into his Land Rover. It was a sturdy SUV, with plenty of space, and it handled the road really well. It made sense why he wanted to drive his vehicle. It was safe and secure.

Alec popped into the boardroom to talk to me, while Ray was making his rounds. He was not too pleased to hear about the incident in the underground garage the day before. He even seemed genuinely concerned.

"I'm really sorry about what happened. I have spoken to security and have requested they walk you to your car in the evenings, when you are working late. Why didn't you call me last night when it happened?"

"Thank you, Alec, but it is unnecessary. Ray will be with me until I move into my office next week. Once I'm settled in there, I will no longer require your boardroom."

"Too bad, I was starting to look forward to seeing you everyday."

"I'm sure you would love to get your boardroom back."

"I'm still wondering why you didn't call me last night."

"You left the office for the evening. It really was not a big deal. It was probably a kid." I explained. "Besides, I don't have your cell number, and your office number wouldn't have done any good."

"Here, pass me your phone. I'll put my cell number into your contacts."

"It's not necessary." I tried to refuse politely.

"I think you should have it, in case you have questions about the merger...or anything else." He took my phone out of my hand and typed in his phone number. I heard his phone beep. "Now I have yours too."

"Thanks." I hesitated because I was not sure this was a good idea.

"Tomorrow I'm having a lunch meeting with some of my financial managers. I think it would be a great idea if you were present."

"Sorry, I can't tomorrow. I'm taking my secretary out to lunch." I hesitated. "I would go but its last minute. Any other time would have been fine." He sighed and looked disappointed. He stared at me briefly with a stern look. I did not want him to blow up the way he did, on my first day. I was always anxious and walked on pins and needles around him.

"Rejected for a second time! I must admit; this does not happen to me very often. In fact, it never does. Most people go out of their way to please me."

"I know how you feel about my role with this merger." I paused. "If you feel it is important, I will reschedule lunch with my secretary." *What is wrong with me?*

He looked at me with a smirk on his face. Oh, he was good at manipulating people. "I understand. This is strike two!" He had an evil smile. "You know what happens if there is a strike three?" I could not tell if he was joking or being serious. Was he threatening me?

Ray knocked and entered the boardroom. He looked at both of us. The tension between us was apparent. Ray chose not to ask any questions. He took a seat and started to read his newspaper and drink his coffee.

"We will discuss this at a later time. I have a meeting to go to."

I was trying to concentrate on the files but found my thoughts filled with the comments Alec had made to me. Alec was a difficult man to read. At times, he was mysterious, but at other times, he was rude and nasty. Then there was a kind side too. Not many people get to witness each side of him. I have seen these sides over the past few days.

I jumped, when my phone beeped with a text notification.

Lunch on Friday!
NO EXCUSES!

Jeez! I knew I would regret him having my cell number. I needed to talk to Carter. It felt like I was cheating on him. It was the third day I had worked out of Alec's office and Carter had no idea. I do not know why I felt I should keep this from him. It was bound to come out, and I wanted it to come from me, instead of hearing it from Ray, Alec, or anybody else.

Carter insisted I stay at his apartment for the rest of the week. He did not want me to be alone at night in my apartment. Carter had always been kind, generous, and caring towards me. He was the only man I had ever trusted. He had always been the first person I would call if I needed anything or had news to share. He had always made time for me, even during busy trials or court cases.

Once we arrived back at Carter's apartment, I assumed Ray would go home. It had been long day for both of us. However, he hung around and inspected the building's security and jotted down some notes on paper, which I assumed was for Carter. I relaxed on the sofa and watched some TV before starting dinner. Lulu snuggled up on my lap and purred. Carter brought her over to his apartment in the morning, along with some of my belongings I needed for the next few days. Lulu was getting older. When I was in university, a classmate had a cat with a litter of six kittens. She was desperately trying to find homes for them. I went look at the cute kittens after class one day. Lulu picked me. She cuddled into the fold of my arm, stayed there, and did not leave. The other kittens played and wrestled with each other. She has been the most gentle, affectionate cat for the last ten years.

My phone started to vibrate with a text message from Carter:

I will be home within the hour.

It was already 7:00. I wrote back:

Making dinner.

Instantly my phone started to vibrate again:

You are spoiling me!

Lulu was not happy I moved her off my lap. She quickly curled up in the corner of the sofa and started cleaning herself. I made spaghetti with Caesar salad and garlic bread. I invited Ray to stay, but he refused. He was meeting his daughter for a late dinner. I admired that quality in him. He loved his daughter to no end. I told him he could leave and meet her, but he said Carter had instructed him to stay with me until he arrived home. He was a respected man in his industry.

It was close to 8:00 p.m. when Carter arrived home. He always had a huge smile on his face, when he greeted me. He put down his briefcase on the ground, gave me a kiss, and lifted me off the ground. "Missed you, how was your day?" he asked.

"It was good. Most of my office is packed," I said proudly.

"Wonderful! Can't wait to have you in my building." He then directed his attention to Ray. "How did everything go? I'm sure you have a list of upgrades."

"I have a list for security upgrades, but I'd like to see the new office to evaluate the security needs there as well," he answered.

"We will be leaving on Friday for the weekend. I can arrange for you to go to the office then. We will be returning on Sunday late afternoon. Do you think it will give you time to arrange any upgrade required for the three locations?"

"I need to grab a few belongings for our weekend away, so maybe tomorrow afternoon we can go to my apartment. I can pack while Ray looks around."

"Sounds like a great idea." Carter smiled. "Would that be fine with you, Ray?"

"Yes, of course," Ray agreed. "It will give me a head start to ensure I have the installment appointments scheduled for the three locations before Sunday evening."

"Actually, Carter, I won't be able to leave early on Friday. My clients asked me to go to a lunch meeting with the financial managers." I looked at Carter. "Maybe during my lunch meeting Ray could look at my new office space."

"I'm not sure it is a good idea."

"Carter, let's not go overboard. I am going to be with a group of people discussing business matters. I think I'll be okay for two hours," I stated. Carter's lips were hard pressed but he nodded okay.

Carter and Ray finished their conversation in Carter's home office. Once Ray left for the evening, we relaxed and started eating dinner. I felt this was the best opportunity to tell him about Alec.

"My merger contract is going well."

"I've been meaning to talk to you about it. Sorry, we have not discussed it; it has been a little chaotic with everything going on this week. Tell me everything." He took a sip of his wine and gave me his attention.

"It's a lot of documents to go through. I'm hoping once I'm in my office I'll be able to concentrate better." I studied Carter.

"You can handle it." He encouraged. "This is a great opportunity for you. Tell me about the partners."

"Well, that's what I wanted to talk to you about." I looked down at my hands nervously. "You know one of the partners."

"Really? Have I represented them before?"

"You know him on a personal level." Carter studied me and waited patiently for me to tell him who he was. "Alec Lockwood."

"What? You have to be kidding." He ran his fingers through his hair out of frustration. "Why are you just telling me now?" His tone in his voice changed.

"I didn't want you to get upset."

"You promised me you'd stay away from him."

"It's complicated. How can I stay away from him when he's one of the merging partners?"

"How? You can walk away from the contract!"

"That is unfair. You know how important this is to my career."

"It's not the last merger. You'll have other opportunities."

"See! I knew you would be upset."

"You don't understand what he is capable of. He doesn't have a good reputation."

"Carter, I barely see him...only once during the day." This was the truth. "And once I'm settled in my new office next week, I won't see him, unless there's a meeting."

"I don't like it. It was not a coincidence for him to be at the dance club and Gala. He was there because of you. He likes to know personal information, to use it against people in the future to blackmail them." He ran his fingers through his hair again. "Maybe it's not a coincidence your windshield was written on, in his office parking garage either!" *I never thought about it. He did leave the office before me.*

"Carter, don't be silly. He does not have any information to use against me. Besides, he's been professional in the office and hasn't made me feel uncomfortable," I lied. I could not tell him, he blew up on me, on the first day and demanded I follow the rules, during the contract. Not to mention, how he threatened strike three would have consequences. I did not understand why I felt I should defend Alec. He was not the ideal person, as a boss. I wanted this merger to be mine. This was my professional goal, and I was not going to let anything stand in my way.

"How could I not see this before? It makes sense. I have been blind-sided, by my personal life. I am not seeing details that are right under my nose. I should have made the connection."

"Sorry you feel that way. I told you, I did not want to risk our friendship. Now we are arguing about a situation not in my control."

"I would still be upset if we were only friends."

Carter's phone started to ring and interrupted our heated conversation. His expression was not pleased. He put his hand over the phone, "I have to take this call. Can we talk about this later?" I nodded my head. My heart began to sink deep into my chest. This was the first time, he did not put me first. He decided his call was more important than resolving our argument.

Chapter Ten

I felt empty inside. Carter and I still had unresolved issues. He did not wake me in the morning. The apartment was quiet. I did not hear him leave for work. He must have been too angry to wake me to say good-bye.

Once I was ready, I headed out to the kitchen, only to find Carter and Ray chatting at the kitchen table. Carter immediately approached me and gave me a hug and a gentle kiss.

"I'm sorry," he whispered.

"I'm sorry too."

"I know it was unfair of me to ask you to walk away from this contract. I trust you. I do not trust him. He has something up his sleeve."

"You have nothing to worry about. So you're okay with me working with him?"

"Not really! However, I also know, I cannot tell you what to do. I want you to be aware and on guard always."

"This merger will be finished in three months...then he won't be an issue."

"It will be the toughest three months. He is always on the prowl to ruin people's lives. He is not a honest man."

"I don't like arguing with you. In seventeen years I can't recall another time we fought." I looked down at my hands. "This merger is important to me but you're more important," I admitted.

"You're important to me too. I want to protect you from people like him. We will get through these next few months." He kissed my forehead and hugged me tight. We stood there for a few minutes in silence.

"You look gorgeous. I think I'm going to have to cancel my meetings, to be with you today." Carter leaned close. "I am getting hard looking at you," he whispered in my ear. Ray was in the kitchen getting a coffee.

"I am glad you like it," I giggled. I wore my baby blue, strapless summer dress with high-heeled shoes. I pulled my hair up into a loose clip to keep my hair off my neck—perfect for a humid day.

"I hope you're not meeting any male clients today looking like that. I think I'd be jealous." He joked but I knew he was referring to Alec.

"I'm taking Sarah out to lunch today." I smiled.

"I think I'm still jealous." He pulled me in tight and kissed me passionately. I felt his hard-on through our clothes. His facial features changed from playful to a sexual sensual look.

"You should have woken me up," I teased. "Now you're going to have to wait to see what I have on, underneath this dress." I made it worse for him. He was growing more intense with desire.

Ray cleared his throat and coughed, as he entered the living room. Carter closed his eyes and frowned at me, before turning around to see Ray. When he turned, he pulled me along with him, so I would be in front of him. He hugged me from behind me, with his hands around my waist. I felt his hard-on against my lower back. Ray was a smart man, he knew.

"Good morning, Miss Brooks." He looked at Carter. "Mr. Blake, Miss Brooks mentioned yesterday, she would like to take Sarah out to lunch today. What are your thoughts?"

"She mentioned it to me, as well." He paused to think for a moment. "I know how much this means to Miss Brooks. Please accompany them to the restaurant, but give them space to enjoy their lunch, privately."

Carter released me and guided me to the table, where my breakfast was waiting for me. He hung around for a few more minutes before leaving. Ray read the newspaper until I was ready to leave. We took his SUV. I read a few emails on the way and then a text came through from Carter:

Having trouble concentrating! LOL

I smiled as I read his text and responded:

Ditto! You looked HOT in your suit, Mr. Blake!

He responded immediately:

Damn! I want you!

I smiled. I loved the way he teased me:

You are being a bad boy, Mr. B.
You should have woken me up this morning! LOL

We were almost at my office. Ray and I did not talk much on the way there. He could see I was busy on my phone. I noticed he glanced over and caught me smiling a few times. "I may be out of line to say this, Miss Brooks, but I have never seen a happier couple than you and Mr. Blake."

"We are happy. Thank you." I smiled. I felt sad for him. I knew he truly missed his wife.

We arrived at my office and everything was as we left it the day before. Ray was precise when he checked the parking lot, office, and surrounding area. I felt safe. A part of me still felt this was unnecessary, but I was enjoying Ray's company. I did not have much to pack, so I finished everything I needed to do by 11:00 a.m. Ray and I sat down and had a coffee together, surrounded by packed boxes, which lined the walls. I spent the last few years in that office. It was where I took the plunge and started my own business. That office holds many memories. A part of me will miss my small office and the friends I have made.

Sarah was almost ready to go to lunch. She was waiting for her backup receptionist to relieve her. I made reservations at a small family owned restaurant. They served a variety of different meals but their specialty was steak or pasta. It was conveniently located across the street from the office. I arranged to have a longer lunchtime for Sarah. I did not want to rush to get her back to the office, within an hour.

Ray walked with us to the restaurant. He sat a few tables away but had a direct view of us. I insisted he eat with us. He refused, saying he did not want to intrude. It crossed my mind that Sarah and Ray would be perfect for each other. I was not a matchmaker, so the thought left my head, as fast as it came.

"Cerise, this is kind of you to take me to lunch."

"It's my pleasure," I smiled at her gently. "You've helped me a lot over these last few years. I could not have done it without you. I wish I could pack you up too and bring you to my new office." I laughed.

"I wish you could too. The office is going to be so dull without you."

"Well, it would be in bad taste if I offered you a job. I know how valuable you are to everyone in the office. It would leave them stranded. You are irreplaceable." I paused, and then smiled at her. "However, if you decided to go elsewhere, make sure you call me first."

"Thank you. It means a lot to me." She smiled sincerely.

We ordered our lunch and a couple glasses of wine. I enjoyed spending time with her. We talked about her son, who was in his second year of university. She was only 24 years old when she was pregnant. It was a one-night stand. Her son did not know his father. She had raised him on her income for all these years. She never married or had a significant other. She joked and admitted, she felt like a virgin because she forgot what it was like to have sex. We both laughed a little too hard when she said that.

"I should set you up with a great guy," I told her looking over at Ray.

"No, I think I'm too old to start the dating game."

"I don't think you're too old. In fact, you do not look your age. You look at least ten years younger than you are."

"Thank you, but enough about me! You have been glowing this week and I saw the articles of you and Mr. Blake." She paused. "So what's the scoop?"

"You noticed."

"You'd have to be stupid not to notice." We laughed.

"Carter and I have been friends for a long time. It is a new experience, for both of us. It feels so right. He makes me happy," I explained.

"I'm happy for you. You deserve it. I have known you for a few years now and I have to say I have not seen you so happy." She lifted up her wine glass. "To happiness and to a new beginning!" We clinked our glasses. I saw Ray watching us from across the room. I could not help notice he looked at Sarah too.

Our lunch arrived. It was delicious. We ordered steak and baked potatoes with steamed vegetables. I glanced over at Ray, and he was eating steak too. We made eye contact and smiled at each other.

Sarah and I continued to laugh and have a good time. We were having coffee and waiting for the bill. I had a gift for Sarah, to thank her for her dedication. I can tell by her reaction, she loved it. I saw it a few weeks ago and thought of her immediately. It has been sitting in the trunk of my car ever since I bought it. I picked it up, thinking I would give it to her as an appreciation gift, which I did from time to time. Who knew my life's path would change in a different direction. Sarah loved to garden and enjoyed her backyard, so I knew she would enjoy the solar ornaments that would light up her garden at night.

"These are beautiful." Tears welled up in her eyes. "You are so kind, you shouldn't have." She smiled. "I have a gift for you too, but it's nothing compared to this." She handed me a beautifully wrapped box.

"Thank you, Sarah." I opened the box to find beautiful earrings. They were tiny silver hoop earrings with a heart that dangled from the bottom. "They're beautiful, Sarah. I love them." I stood up from my seat to give her a hug. We embraced for a moment. I could see Ray getting ready to jump up from his seat too.

I sat down again and stared at the beautiful earrings. I decided to wear them. I took out the earrings I was wearing and put on the new ones.

"They are beautiful on you. Especially with your hair pulled up," Sarah complimented.

"Thank you."

Our server arrived with our bill and asked, "By chance are you Miss Brooks?"

"Yes, I am," I replied.

"The woman crossing the road, asked me to give this to you." She pointed out the window to a woman wearing black, with a hoodie over her head. She briefly stopped at a car; exchanged something through the window, and then they both parted in opposite directions.

"Thank you," My heart started to flutter with nervousness. The server continued on her way to the next table. I made eye contact with Ray. He immediately came over to our table. I explained to him what I saw and pointed to the black envelope on the table.

"May I open it for you?" Ray asked. I nodded.

Ray put on rubber gloves and opened it carefully. When he slid out the card, the word 'TO', was written in red lipstick, on plain white card stock. My heart sank. I started to panic. I tried to remain calm so Sarah would not ask too many questions, or get scared or worry.

"Ray, lets pay our bills and take Sarah back to the office." I paused and looked at Sarah. "It was so wonderful to have lunch with you today. I'm going to miss you." I stood up and gave her a tight hug. A few tears rolled down my face. I cried out of fear at this point, but Sarah thought my tears were because of our good-bye.

Ray paid our bills and escorted us out, across the street, and to the office. Sarah returned to work and Ray and I returned to his parked car. He was even more cautious and protective than usual. When I sat in the car, I cried uncontrollably. I pulled my knees up to my chest and hugged them. Ray let me cry. He did not try to console me. I think he knew I needed to cry, to let out my emotions. He called Carter on his Bluetooth. I could only hear Ray's side of the conversation. I knew he was taking instruction from Carter. They hung up and a moment later, my phone rang. I knew it was Carter from call display on my phone.

"Hello." I sniffed.

"Cerise, are you okay?"

"I don't know, I'm shaking! Why is this happening?" I asked.

"I'm leaving the office. I'm going to meet you at your apartment," he explained.

"Okay." I felt better knowing I was going to see him soon.

We were around the corner from my apartment. Ray parked in my parking spot. Before coming around to my side of the vehicle to let me out, he investigated around some bushes. He returned to me and escorted me upstairs. I opened my door to my apartment. I cried, "No!" and fell to the ground. Ray pulled out his gun and checked out my apartment.

My apartment was small. It was a one-bedroom condominium with two bathrooms, a living room, and a kitchen. I decorated my apartment with leather and oak furniture. I had hard wood floors throughout my condominium, and painted the walls with warm dark taupe colors. I had many plants scattered and strategically placed throughout my apartment. My fireplace was my focal point when you opened the front door. I had pictures on the mantel with my beautiful mirror above it.

I could not breath. The adrenaline was making my heart race. My hands were shaking. I sobbed, sitting on the floor at the entrance. *Why would anybody do this?* I did not understand. *Was I having a nightmare?* For the first time in my life, my life was starting to fall into place. I was in love with my best friend, who treated me with respect, kindness, and love. My career was looked bright, with a huge contract and a beautiful new office. Yet, an unknown person was stalking and threatening me. *Why Me?*

I looked around my living room through my tears in disbelief. The pictures that were on my mantle were on the floor, smashed. My beautiful plants had been tipped over, leaving dirt everywhere on the hardwood flooring. You could see the footprints of dirty shoes, tracked throughout my apartment. It looked like a man's size shoe.

I could hear Ray's footsteps walking room to room. He was trying not to disturb any evidence. He knew my apartment would soon be busy with detectives looking for clues. The leather sofas had white filling popping out through the large slashes, made by a knife. The rooms in my sight were touched and destroyed, in one way or another. I could not see my bedroom but I assumed it was the same. Even the kitchen dishes were broken on the floor. The kitchen cupboards were open with nothing in them. A couple of the cupboard doors were hanging by one hinge.

The only thing not destroyed, was the mirror over my fireplace mantel. The word "NEEDS" was written on the mirror, in red lipstick. It was screaming at me.

"Miss Brooks, I need you to breathe. Take a deep breath," he instructed. "You have to be strong." He was taking deep breaths with me.

I heard footsteps in the hallway coming towards my apartment. I jumped when my door swung open. It was Carter. He fell to the ground and hugged me, pulled my head to his chest and rocked me back and forth. "It's okay! It's okay!" He paused and silently mouthed some words to Ray, then returned his attention to me, "I'm here, I'm here." He rubbed my arms to sooth me.

"My apartment is trashed. Why?" I cried.

"I don't have the answers. We will find the person responsible for this. Trust me." Carter promised. "Kyle and Scott are on their way. I know they will have questions for you, but I want to get you out of this apartment, sooner than later."

"What about my clothes? Pictures of my mom?" I started to ramble.

Moments later Kyle and Scott arrived. They started writing a report. They had a team come in and take pictures and search for fingerprints. They knew they would not find fingerprints other than Carter's and mine. Whoever was responsible, was smart enough to wear gloves. Kyle turned over a leather chair in its up-tight position, for me to sit in. They asked me many questions. Some of them seemed repetitive. I asked if it was okay to use my bathroom while they were still investigating. Once I was in the bathroom after excusing myself, I sat there thinking. *Why was this happening? I tried to think of who would do this. Could it really be the jealous ex-girlfriend, Nicole?*

I glanced up, looked towards the door, and noticed a hole drilled at the bottom of the handle. It was not the first time I seen one like it. Memories started to come back to me, of when I was sixteen years old.

Tony drilled peepholes, under each door handle, in the townhouse. He would watch me, when I was in the bathroom or dressed in my bedroom. Even in the spare bedroom, where I hung out with my friends. My mother caught him spying on me through the peephole, while I was in the bathroom. He was jerking off outside the door, and he did not hear my mom coming up the stairs. There was a huge outbreak. They fought a long time that night. It ended with my mom getting a black eye. I heard my mom say, "You were jerking off looking at my daughter through that hole! You are sick!" She sobbed and yelled at him in anger.

He responded, "Are you jealous?" It was then, I saw the hole for the first time in my life. I was instantly embarrassed. I was a curious sixteen years old virgin. I was spread eagle sitting on the edge of the bathtub, pleasuring myself, as I watched with a compact mirror. The drilled hole had a direct view of the bathtub and my position. I remember looking through the hole, the next day, to see the view for myself and it was a 'perfect view'. I did not tell my mom what I was doing behind the door that night. I think it would have killed her to know. I should have told my mom. Maybe she would have left him. He managed to wiggle his way out of the situation with a lies, promises, and showered her with flowers, cards, and gifts.

I jumped when Carter knocked on the door. I was in my own world thinking of the past. "Cerise, are you okay?"

"Yes, I'm fine. I'll be out in a minute," I answered.

When I came out of the bathroom, Carter was standing there waiting for me. He gave me a gentle kiss. "We can go home now. They don't need us here anymore," he whispered. "Is there anything you want to take with us?"

"Someone's hands have been all over my clothes. I feel violated. I need clothes but most of all, I want the picture of my mom: The one with both of us, at Niagara Falls. It should be on my dresser." The picture was very special to me. It was the last picture I had of us together, before she passed. Mom decided we needed a girl's weekend together. It was great. One of my mom's friends had to back out of her weekend plans, due to a family emergency. She offered my mom the Niagara Falls package deal. It was too late to get her money refunded and she knew mom could not afford a weekend getaway, so she gifted the package deal to my mom and I.

"You sit here and I will gather a few items." He received permission to grab a few possessions and returned with my luggage full of clothes, and then we left. Phillip drove us back to Carter's apartment. He had been waiting patiently. Carter was lucky to have Phillip as his right-hand man. Ray followed closely behind our vehicle, back to Carter's apartment. I was exhausted. It was 7:00 p.m. It was 1:30 p.m. when I received the black envelope at the restaurant and around 2:00 p.m. when I walked in to my apartment. I was an emotionally drained. My stomach growled but I did not have an appetite.

I sat on Carter's sofa, curled up with a blanket for close to an hour. Lulu curled up with me. It was as if she knew how I felt. I could hear Carter, Ray, and Phillip talking about leaving for the weekend and what they were responsible for, while we were away. *I cannot leave tonight! I have my meeting tomorrow! I cannot get a strike three!* I thought.

"Carter, I can't leave tonight for the cottage."

"Cerise, I think its best to get you out of here. You have had two messages in one day and the first note from Monday. You're not safe here."

"Carter, I can't. I have made a commitment to this merger. I don't want to come across as unprofessional." I rubbed my temples with my fingers. "We can leave right after work tomorrow."

"Ever since you started this merger everything has gone to hell. I have my suspicions."

"Carter, I'm already behind a day. I should have been working today. Everything is too much; the merger, packing my office, working long hours, living here, and you! My head is spinning out of control." I looked up at the ceiling to hold back the tears. "I need to spend the day at my clients' office tomorrow to catch up on time missed today, then go to my lunch meeting. I also need to face my apartment and go through my belongings and clean it up."

Carter looked frustrated and concerned. "That's why going away this weekend is necessary. You've had a stressful week."

"I'm really scared. I do not understand any of this. A part of me wants nothing more than to run away from these problems, but it's not who I am." I began to cry. Ray and Phillip were sitting at the kitchen table listening and had sympathetic looks on their faces.

"Come here, Ma Cerise." Carter sat down beside me and pulled me closer to sit on his lap. I snuggled into his shoulder. "It's going to be okay. Kyle is looking after everything on his end. And I'm going to look after you."

Chapter Eleven

I was up with the birds Friday morning. I had so much to accomplish. My plan was to go to Alec's office first thing and tackle some of the files before the business lunch meeting. I was at the office by 7:30 a.m. Ray had stayed the night at Carter's apartment; it made it easier to get up early and get a head start to my day.

Carter had arranged to have a cleaning crew go to my apartment and start cleaning up the broken glass, dishes, and plant soil, which was throughout my apartment. I was grateful Carter was so supportive. We had agreed to meet at my apartment late afternoon. He told me he would help go through my belongings and organize my apartment.

"You're here bright and early this morning," Alec said as he entered the boardroom. I nodded. "I bought you a coffee. You look like you need it."

"Thank you." I took the coffee from his hands and took a sip.

"Want to talk about it?"

"Nothing to talk about."

"If you change your mind, you know where to find me." He was about to leave but instead, walked over to where I was sitting and started to massage my shoulders. My body tensed to his touch. His hands felt so good. I dropped my head slightly forward and closed my eyes.

"I can feel the stress in your shoulders." His hands worked their way up my neck. "I can help relieve your stress in more ways than you think." His tone in his voice was soft and sexy. I opened my eyes wide and stood up. I could not let this happen. I could not go anywhere...I was trapped. Alec had me cornered between the table, chair, and boxes of files, which were stacked on top of each other. Alec was so close I could smell his cologne and his mouthwash on his breath.

"Thanks for the reminder... I have to make an appointment for a massage. It will help."

"No appointment necessary. You can ask me any time."

"I'm sure my massage therapist will do fine."

We both heard someone walking down the hall towards the boardroom. Alec immediately backed off and walked to a box of files, pretending to be looking for something. To my relief, it was Ray who walked in the boardroom. Shortly thereafter, Alec left claiming he had a meeting.

❈

As planned, Ray was going to inspect my new office for a security system, while I was at my meeting. The meeting was at a Thai restaurant, a block away from the building. I walked down the block towards the restaurant. Even in broad daylight, I had an eerie feeling, someone was watching me. I looked down one of the alleys as I passed it and noticed a homeless person sitting there staring at me, from underneath his baseball cap. I walked faster and looked over my shoulder a few times, especially if someone walked behind me at a faster pace. I walked into the restaurant, expecting it to be busy. Nobody was there. I must have had the wrong restaurant. I was about to turn around to leave, when a waiter came from the back and asked, "Are you Miss Brooks?"

"Yes, I am."

"Your table reservation is at the back, please follow me." He grabbed a couple of menus and walked towards the back of the restaurant. I followed him. He led me to an area of the restaurant, which was a private area away from the rest of the dining area. When we turned the corner, I saw Alec. He was alone. He stood up to greet me and helped push my chair in, when I sat down.

"So lovely to see you outside of the office and without your bodyguard."

"Alec, I thought this was a meeting with the financial managers!"

"That was yesterday."

"I thought you rescheduled it for today?"

"What would give you that impression?"

"Well, for starters you said, it would be important for me to meet them."

"Sorry you had that impression. I only asked you out for lunch."

"What about the strike three crap?"

He looked firmly at me. He was so hard to read. Was he going to blow a fuse?

"Listen, I wanted to go to lunch. Nothing more! I didn't think you would go with me if you didn't think it was for a meeting."

"You got that right." I stood up to leave. "I have too much work to do. I don't have time to play head games."

"You leave, its strike three."

"So you're going to hold strike three over my head for the whole entire time?"

"It seems to be working for me so far."

"Well, it's not working for me." I sat down. I leaned over the table towards him and firmly said. "You use strike three with me again, and I'm gone. As far as I am concerned, you will be the one to strike out when I leave. You know I'm the best person for this job."

"Love those fighting words," he laughed in my face. "I never strike out."

"You know what? I will have lunch with you...only to find out what's your problem."

"There we go...now we're talking."

The waiter came back to pour our wine. He took our order and vanished into the kitchen.

"Why isn't anybody here?"

"I reserved the whole restaurant. I didn't want anybody to see us together and get the wrong idea."

"How thoughtful of you!"

"I usually get what I want. You should know that by now."

"And what do you want?"

"For starters, I want you. Ever since I saw you at the dance club a week ago today."

"You're making this business relationship difficult and awkward."

"It doesn't have to be."

"But it is awkward. I have no interest in anything more with you. I'm with Carter."

"I think differently. I think you are attracted to me. I see it in your eyes. The way you tense when you are around me. The way you cannot look into my eyes. You know sex will come eventually. I prefer sooner."

"You're so full of yourself. You make me uncomfortable! That's why I get tense and don't look into your eyes."

"Lie to yourself all you want, but I know the truth."

"Changing the subject now...why don't you like Carter?"

"Why don't you ask him?"

"Cause I'm asking you."

"Let's just say, when I was a kid, everyone always made me feel I had to be better than him. My parents, teachers, and coaches you name it. Now that we are adults and I am better than he is, he cannot handle it. I am more successful than he is, richer than he is and I always get the girl."

"I understand it now. I am a game to you. Let me save you the hassle. I will not leave Carter for you. You may have several multi-million dollar companies, you may be richer than he is, but you will never be better than Carter. He is more of a man, than you could ever hope to be." I stood up and left.

I could not stay in the office any longer. I grabbed my computer and briefcase and left the building. I hailed down a cab and headed to my apartment. Traffic was usually slow in Downtown Toronto on any day of the week, but on that particular Friday afternoon, it seemed to be going at a snail's pace. I stared out the window, as the taxi drove past the Thai restaurant. To my surprise, Alec was leaving the restaurant. He made eye contact with me, smiled, and blew me an arrogant air kiss.

I called Ray to let him know I would be at my apartment cleaning up. He still had a few miscellaneous items to finish, at my new office. He knew Carter would not like my sudden change in plans. However, I did not give him much of an option—I needed to leave immediately. I opened my apartment door slowly. My heartbeat raced as I walked in. I could hear some music playing and some rattling of broken glass in my kitchen. I expected to see the staff from the cleaning company. I jumped when Carter's head popped up from underneath the counter.

"What a surprise! What are you doing here? I wasn't expecting you until much later."

"I was able to leave early. The lunch meeting was canceled." I smiled. "What are you doing here?"

"Well, I thought I'd get a head start. The cleaning crew left to get lunch. They will be back in an hour."

"You are always so sweet." I walked into his arms and gave him a huge hug, then kissed him passionately. If only he knew, how much I loved him. The feeling I had inside when I was around him, made me realize, I was the luckiest woman alive.

He was not thrilled I took a taxi back to my apartment. However, he was happy I was with him for the afternoon. We cleaned my apartment together. Most of my belongings had to be disposed of and brought down to the garbage bins, at the back of the building. Phillip helped Carter move the large furniture to the garbage bins. Once the damaged belongings were disposed of, my apartment echoed.

In my living room, I had one leather chair, a coffee table, and my area rug. My mirror still hung over my fireplace mantel, minus the red lipstick. My kitchen only had cutlery and some plastic bowls and containers. My bedroom was not too bad, as far as damage. My bed and dresser were fine. The mirror, attached to my dresser, was destroyed. My clothes were thrown around the room. Carter helped me go through my clothes. We refolded them and put them in the dresser or hung them back on hangers, in the closet. He was a little frisky and playful when going through my panties. As usual, he was able to make the best of the situation and make me laugh. I was so grateful Carter hired a cleaning crew. They not only cleaned up the broken pieces, they swept, mopped, and washed down the surfaces. My apartment was somewhat back to normal. At least it was clean and organized.

Cleaning my apartment was the best part of my day. No matter what we did, it was always fun being together. I did not want to go back to my apartment anytime soon. For now, I was going to stay where I felt safe...with Carter.

Chapter Twelve

The road was bumpy, on the way to Carter's cottage. It was deep in the woods and isolated. It was so peaceful and tranquil. Carter's jeep handled the off road conditions well. Carter loved his cars. For as long as I have known Carter, he always had a Jeep. It suited him. It was sexy, strong, and reliable.

"Almost there," he informed.

"I can't wait. It's been so long since I've been there."

"It's been awhile for me too. I think it was three years ago, everyone came up as a group. Remember, everyone came up for the Canada Day long-weekend. We were celebrating the start up of your business. It was a fun weekend. As I recall you were all over me," he joked.

"No, you were all over me. I remember Sam and Becky asking me... '*Are you guys doing each other?*' ..." I smiled.

"We did come close that weekend to having sex for the first time. Do you remember? We were in the boathouse when Kyle came in to get a life jacket." Carter laughed.

"I know, how embarrassing. I still remember Kyle's laughter, when he left the boathouse. Shortly after, everyone started yelling from the dock *'Carter, are you coming yet? We want to go boating!'* How could I forget?" I laughed. "Do they still tease you about that?"

"They sure do. I think teasing me is their goal in life," he laughed. "The joke was on me. You were wearing your bikini cover-up and I had taken your bikini bottoms off. I was so hard. I wanted you badly. My hand was up your cover-up when Kyle walked in. So close but no cigar," He smiled, and stared out the windshield.

"Then we left that afternoon to go home." We were silent for a few minutes. I could not help wonder what our lives would be like if that weekend would have been different. I touched his hand, which was on the stick shift. "Thank you for bringing me here this weekend."

"My pleasure," he smiled.

We arrived. It was so dark out you could barely see your hand in front of your face. The stars were bright and sparkling by the millions.

Carter left his Jeep headlights on and aimed them at the front porch. He jumped out and opened the cottage door, then turned on the porch lights. He returned to the Jeep, turned the ignition off, and grabbed our bags. We walked in the cottage together. He closed and locked the door behind us out of habit.

It was beautiful. It was not really a cottage. It was a home on a lake. It had four bedrooms, decorated in different themes. It was an open concept design with the kitchen, living room, and dining room in a large open room, with wall-to-wall windows over-looking the lake. It was perfect for entertaining. It had high ceilings with oak beams and hardwood flooring throughout. The cottage was up on a hill and had a zigzag cedar staircase leading down to the boathouse and dock. The exterior siding and stairs was a beautiful cedar color. There was a huge deck attached to the cottage, with beautiful exterior furniture for dining, lounging, and barbequing.

I sat down on the comfortable sofa and put my feet up. I was not tired anymore, since I slept for a couple of hours in the Jeep. I was relaxed. September was approaching, and the nights were getting cooler. I watched Carter build the fire in the wood stove. He had defined arm and back muscles, which were bulging, through his tight T-shirt. He sat beside me and put his arm behind me. I snuggled into him. He shifted over so we were both lying down on the sofa. My fingers were playing with his nipple through his T-shirt.

"This is the best part of my day."

"You must be tired. It was a long drive." I said. "A long day, too."

"I'm not too bad. I'm happy I'm here with you."

I looked up at him and smiled. "It's our one week anniversary."

"I was thinking the same thing." He kissed my forehead.

"Maybe I'm too much trouble. How many times this week did you, have to leave work early or go in late, because of me? How much stress can I stir up? I have put you through so much this week, it's enough to steer you in the opposite direction." I did not want to be a needy girlfriend.

"Ma Cerise, none of that matters to me. I would still do the same even if we were only friends. That's what you do for people you love unconditionally." He shifted our bodies again, so I was lying on top of him. "Besides, I'm happy."

I leaned down and started to kiss him. His hands were exploring every inch of me from my shoulders, to my back, and over my derriere. I felt him growing under me. I was lost in the moment. He held my ass and rubbed his cock into me, through our clothes.

"You're so sexy in these tight jeans," he said between kisses.

"These old jeans?" I asked, giggling.

"It's not the jeans, it's what's underneath that makes them sexy on you." He pushed harder into me. "What are you wearing underneath?" He started to push my jeans down over my hips. I was wearing boy shorts with a matching bra, under my jeans and T-shirt. I had put iron-on letters on the front and back of my panties, a few days prior. The front said, 'I'M' in white.

"Interesting... 'I'M' what?" he asked. I turned over on my belly so he could see the back. "Carter's... I'm Carter's." He smiled ear to ear. "That you are, Ma Cerise." He smacked my ass playfully. He slid my legs off the sofa so I was kneeling on the floor facing the sofa. He was kneeling with his chest touching my back. He pulled my panties down my thighs to my knees. He felt my heat between my legs.

"You are wet for me, Cerise." He unzipped his jeans to free his cock. He rubbed the head of his cock against my opening. He entered slowly. I moaned. With a few slow pushes, he filled me. I squeezed my muscles to tighten around him.

"You're so tight." He started to fuck me harder, holding my hips. He was so deep. His balls smacked against me, each time he slammed into me. He pulled off my T-shirt over my head and unclasped my bra. With both hands, he played with my breasts and nipples. He pulled out of me and turned me over to my back. My head leaned back on the cozy cushions. I watched him take off his T-shirt. I could not take my eyes off his muscular chest and arms. He was so strong, yet so gentle. He pulled me closer to the edge of the sofa and put his cock back inside of me. We watched each other's facial expressions. He held me tight to grind deep into me. Watching him pleasure me was sexy. I moaned. I could not hold on any longer. I closed my eyes, arched my back, and let my orgasm take me into the twilight zone. He bent down, sucked, and kissed my nipples. He pumped faster, until he came inside of me. I watched his facial expression turn from sexy, to intense, and back to sexy and then fulfilled.

He grabbed a blanket, which was lying on the back of the sofa and covered both of us. The lights were dim and the fire crackled. I almost forgot about my problems.

90

Chapter Thirteen

I was a little disoriented Saturday morning. It took me a second to realize where I was. I was in Carter's bedroom, at the cottage. I did not remember going to his bed. Carter must have transferred me there, after I fell asleep on the sofa. The blinds blocked most of the morning light from shining through. You could see dust particles floating in the air, in the beam of light, which peaked through the side of the blind. Carter was still sleeping beside me. I decided to let him sleep. He had had a long day the day before and then drove three hours to get to the cottage.

I tiptoed out of the bedroom naked, closing the door behind me. The door creaked slightly at the hinges. I walked to the bathroom, found a terry robe, and put it on. I had no idea where my overnight bag was, or my clothes from the night before. I assumed they would still be over by the sofa. I puttered around the kitchen trying to find tea bags and mugs. I started a pot of coffee for Carter and made myself a tea. I walked out to the deck and sat on the lounge chair. I loved the view of the lake from this spot. The lake was calm. There was not a cloud in the sky. It was so quiet and yet so noisy. The birds were singing, the branches cracked from time to time, and I could hear boat motors on the lake, in the distance. It was a beautiful orchestra to my ears.

Carter greeted me warmly, as he walked on the deck, with a coffee in his hand. His jeans hung low on his hips. I admired his shirtless chest, six-pack, and V line. Moments earlier I was enjoying the tranquil view and sounds of the cottage's surroundings, until Carter walked out. His body was a distraction and my focus changed to his V line. It has been years since I had had sex. I did not give it much thought, until Carter and I had sex for the first time. I could not look at him the same way…he was delicious.

"It's so beautiful this morning," I smiled.

"I often wonder what you think about when you sit out here, drinking your tea." He sat down next to me. "You sit in this exact spot, each time you come up to the cottage."

"I guess I love the beauty and peacefulness I hear and see here. Life is so simplified," I explained.

"It's a great place to get away. My parents loved bringing my brothers and I here throughout the years. My mom says it is not the same anymore. She says children brought this place to life. I think she says that because she wants grandchildren." Carter chuckled.

"Do you think your brothers will have children one day?" I asked.

"Dalton and Vanessa have been trying but they are having difficulty," he explained, referring to his older brother. "Vanessa has had two miscarriages and they have been trying to get pregnant again for a year now. We try not to bring it up anymore."

"I'm so sorry to hear that. Do you think they will try in-vitro?"

"That's what they are trying now. I think they would be great parents." He looked down at his coffee mug.

"I think they would be too. I am sure good things will happen soon for them," I tried to be positive. "What about Preston? Is he dating anyone?"

"Preston is playing the field. There hasn't been anyone special enough, to bring home to mom yet." he smiled.

"Do you want children?" I asked.

"I did not plan to have children because of my career." He paused and looked deep into my eyes. "Until recently...Lately I have been thinking about having a family of my own." he smiled shyly.

"Is that right? What has brought this on?" I asked teasingly.

"A special girl I have been in love with for years," he admitted.

"Really? I'd love to meet her."

"I can arrange that." He leaned over the lounge chair and kissed me. "What about you? Do you see yourself having children?" he asked seriously.

"Yes, I always imagined I would have two." I looked at Carter. "But I'm getting older. I always told myself, if it does not happen before thirty-five, I will not have any."

"What about marriage?" Carter asked seriously.

"Yes, I'm a girl. I want the happily ever after." I looked across the lake. This conversation was getting serious but I really wanted to know how he felt about commitment and family. "What about you?"

"Are you asking me to marry you?" he asked with a huge smile.

I swatted at his arm.

"There's only one person I would marry," he admitted. "I think you know that already."

"Really? I'd love to meet her," I joked.

Carter started to tickle me into submission, but I would not give up easily. I escaped from his hold and ran through the sliding doors to the kitchen. Carter was behind me, chasing me. He grabbed me, lifted me in his arms, and kissed me. He slid the robe off my shoulders and let it drop on the kitchen floor.

"I have never had sex in this kitchen before." He unzipped his jeans and dropped them. We stood there touching and kissing each other's bodies playfully. I turned around to face the counter. I held onto the counter for balance and bent over slightly so my ass rubbed his cock. I tilted my head to look over my shoulder at him with my 'fuck me' look.

"I have never met anyone like you before." He smiled and rubbed his cock on my bare bottom. My blood started to rush faster with excitement. He knelt down and stroked my arousal with his tongue. He knew the exact spot to send shivers throughout my body. He touched my sensitive spot and made my body jerk with desire. He stood up, grabbed his cock, and pushed it in my opening, filling me inside. He pounded into me hard. With each hard thrust, I had to reposition myself to remain balanced. He stopped, to my disappointment.

He opened the fridge and grabbed a few items. He spread the robe out on the floor and guided me down. I lied down and waited to see what he was up to. He knelt down above me, balanced on his hands and knees. His muscular body leaned over me, and then he kissed my lips. My body was screaming for him, to put his cock back inside of me. He leaned back on his feet. My legs rested over his. He reached for one of the cans he took out of the fridge and squirted the whipped cream onto my body, then on his. The coldness sent a shiver through me. The sweet smell filled the air. My nipples hardened even more with the coldness. His playfulness made me giddy.

"Do you want chocolate or caramel?" he offered.

"Both?"

He squirted the chocolate and caramel over both of us. There was something sexy about Carter naked, in the kitchen, covered with sundae toppings.

"Nutritional breakfast!" I said sarcastically.

He had already started to kiss, suck, and lick the toppings off my breasts. He responded with "Hmm hum." We were gooey and sticky. He moved around my body to my head and leaned over to lick my sensitive spot. His huge, hard cock was in my face. I started to lick the toppings from his shaft. Whipped cream, chocolate, and caramel covered us—face, neck, hair, and body. Once I licked him clean, I put his cock in my mouth and sucked it. I rubbed my lips aggressively over every inch of his cock. He would pause occasionally, when I put his cock down my throat.

We changed positions. I stood on all fours and he put his cock into me from behind. The floor was sticky from the mess we created. He pulled my hips tight against him and moaned aloud, as he came inside of me.

Carter helped me up off the floor and hugged me in our state of stickiness. "We need to take a shower." We showered together in the bathroom. My bikini and cover-up was the only thing I needed. I left my hair down and wet, to dry naturally. I did not bother styling my hair. I knew it would get wet again, when we swam in the lake later. Carter put on his swim trunks too. He left his hair wet and fingered combed through it.

I cleaned up the floor, while Carter started to make breakfast. He made pancakes with blueberries. We ate breakfast on the deck and enjoy the beautiful, hot summer morning.

"This is delicious."

"It's really the only meal I know how to make," he laughed. "I'm glad you like it."

"I do... I'm curious, how come there's food here in the fridge?" I asked.

"Mom was up here for a couple of days, with her girlfriends. When I told her I was going to bring you up here, she bought groceries. She headed back to the city yesterday morning."

"She's always been caring and nurturing. You're lucky to have such a wonderful mom."

"Yes, I know." He was silent for a moment. "She's the glue that holds this family together. You know she has always considered you the daughter she never had."

"I know. She has been a huge part of my life. I don't know what I would have done without her after..." I did not want to ruin our morning by bringing up my past. "What will she think of me now...stealing her golden boy away?" I asked seriously.

"Secretly, I think she's planning our wedding. The invites have already been sent out."

"So when's the big day?"

"Are you asking me to marry you again?" he teased playfully.

I sat on his lap. "Is this what married life would be like with you?" I kissed him gently.

"Yes, only better," he whispered through our joined lips. "I would marry you today, if you'd agree to it. We have known each other for seventeen years. I know it's only been one week, as an official couple, but I have known for years you were the one for me."

"The feeling is mutual. I forced those romantic thoughts out of my head because I did not want to ruin our friendship." I put my forehead on his. "I have been missing out all these years."

"Good things come to those who wait."

I forgot about my problems with my stalker, trashed apartment, Alec, and the stress of moving into my new office on Monday. We really enjoyed our time together alone. We spent time on the boat, touring around looking at properties, swimming, and diving off the dock, and sun tanning. It was our little paradise, secluded from the rest of the world.

Usually, I would push people away if they tried to get serious. With Carter, I was confident and comfortable. It scared me a little. This was new for me. I wanted more with Carter. Then a part of me felt we rushed our relationship. I was living in his apartment. We had explored each other bodies in so many ways. We had talked about our future, marriage, and children. *Did we rush in to a relationship? Possibly, we were slow getting to that point, after seventeen years.*

Our weekend passed quickly. We had to go to Carter's parents house for a family lunch. I was a little nervous about going. I had been there a hundred times, but not as Carter's girlfriend.

I decided to look at my texts and emails during the drive home. I received a number of texts from Sam and Becky. Both were worried about me. I guessed Kyle must have told Sam, who then told Becky about what happened on Thursday. I texted them both back and gave them an update of where I was, for the weekend. I told them, I would call when we arrived home. I had some business emails to take care of as well. I set up a few appointments in my new office for the following week. There was a text from Alec as well.

He was arrogant. I deleted the text immediately. It was not necessary to respond. I definitely did not want Carter seeing the text message from him. I considered changing my cell number. The harassment was getting out of control.

A couple of hours flew by—I realized Carter and I had not talked, while I worked.

"I'm sorry for being so busy on my phone."

"That's okay. I had you to myself, without any interruptions, the entire weekend," he replied. I admired his understanding. Men I have dated in the past could not deal with me being an ambitious professional businessperson. I found men to be intimidated or jealous of my success.

"I had an amazing weekend with you. We should do it again soon." I smiled.

"I was thinking next weekend we should have a party on our yacht. Kyle, Sam, Becky, and Mike...it would be fun! There's enough room for everyone to sleep too."

"Sounds like a great idea. I hope it is Kyle's weekend off. I'd love to have everyone together." I always enjoyed it when everyone spent time together. "I wonder if Lulu will like it on the yacht?"

"I'm sure she will, as long as you're there."

"I hope Ray and Phillip took good care of her this weekend. You know how angry she gets if she does not get her soft food in the morning."

Chapter Fourteen

We were thirty minutes away from Carter's parents house, so I touched up my makeup in the mirror and sprayed some perfume on my neck and wrists. Carter was organized. He packed my dress and shoes to wear to the lunch. I would not have thought about it, with the events on Thursday and Friday. We would have had to go to Carter's apartment to change first, instead of going directly to his parent's house, for lunch. He picked out my navy summer dress with polka dots on it. It opened into a flared skirt, from my waist to above my knee. My navy pumps matched perfectly. Carter wore beige cotton pants, a short sleeve button down shirt, and his loafers.

The butterflies in my stomach started going crazy before we pulled up into the driveway.

"You look nervous," Carter observed.

"I am. I don't know why."

"Don't worry. You know everyone already, and I will be with you." He touched my hand and caressed it. His touch sent a warm energy up my arm. It was instantly calming.

"Who's going to be here today?"

"My parents and brothers," he answered.

He walked over to my side of the car and opened the door for me. He took my hand in his and walked towards the door. He gave my hand a little squeeze, and then gave me a quick kiss on my forehead. He opened the door to allow me in first. I stepped inside the Blake's' beautiful family home.

"SURPRISE!"

I jumped back into Carter's chest. "Happy Birthday!" he said with a huge smile. *What? A Surprise Party?* My face began to blush and it took everything to hold back the tears.

Hannah and Savannah ran towards me. They were Samantha and Kyle's five-year-old twin daughters. I loved it when they greeted me with hugs and kisses. I gave them each hugs and asked them, "Did you know about this surprise party?" I raised my eyebrow and put my hand on my hip.

"Yep! We weren't allowed tell you," they sang in unison. I gave them another hug and complimented them on their dresses.

"Happy Birthday, Cerise. I hope you were surprised." Samantha greeted me with a hug. "I told you last week, we'd have to plan a Pool Party and BBQ, so technically I wasn't hiding anything from you," she laughed.

"Considering my birthday was three weeks ago, yes, I'm very surprised," I replied.

Kyle gave me a hug. Then they took their kids out to the backyard so the other guests could say their hellos. I was surprised to see my friends. I did not have any family, so I always considered my friends my family. Phillip, Ray and Sarah were also there, and a few of my university friends, as well.

"Sorry, I was the decoy to mislead you into thinking it was a family lunch today," Mrs. Blake admitted. "I'm glad you were surprised."

"It worked for sure. Thank you."

"I had nothing to do with it." She looked over at her son. "It was Carter's doing. I just invited you to your surprise party," she smiled.

"I don't know if my son ever works," Mr. Blake joked. "He is always planning something." He gave me a hug and whispered in my ear, "Happy belated birthday, Sweetheart."

After everyone greeted me at the entrance, we proceeded to the backyard. The backyard garden was beautiful. It had the in-ground pool with a waterfall in one corner, which splashed in the pool. The grassy area had beautiful hedges and flowers along the edges. The tables were set up under a tented canopy. There was soft music playing in the background. Carter hired a catering crew for the BBQ. They were at the end of the tented area.

It was casual and relaxed. Some people were swimming in the pool. I could see Kyle in the water playing with Hannah and Savannah. Samantha was on the side of the pool with her feet dipped in. Her highlights looked beautiful against her brown hair. Her hazel eyes popped out against her tanned skin.

I could see Rebecca and Mike sitting at one of the tables. I only met Mike the night of the Gala and it was a busy night, so we did not have the chance to talk. I joined them at their table. They were so happy I came over to talk to them. We chatted for a while. Mike was kind. I knew he was falling hard and fast, for Becky. She was hypnotizing, with her long, red, curly hair and green eyes. She was a model and acted in plays and musicals. Mike was the owner of the dance club, Midnight House. His partner ran the operations side of the business. He was at the dance club by chance, the last time we were there. His partner had an emergency that evening, so he filled in for the night. Sometimes things happen for a reason. If he did not fill in for his partner, he would not have met Becky. They looked so happy together.

"Guess what?" Becky sounded excited.

"What?" I asked.

"I have this new part in a play called 'Anything Goes.' We are going to start rehearsals soon. The show will be in production, next year," she explained. "It's a love story which takes place on a ship with singing sailors. I have one of the female lead roles."

"That's wonderful! I can't wait to see you in it." I gave her a hug. She was so talented. I kept telling her one-day she would make it big. She almost gave up on her dream a few times. It was challenging to land the lead movie roles. Whenever she felt like walking away from her dream, something pulled her back in. She would get a major modeling contract or acting role.

I managed to speak with all of my guests. I was truly happy to see everyone. Everyone seemed to be having a great time. There were many children running around and playing organized games, which were scattered around the backyard. Carter thought of everything. Even a clown, making animal balloons, for the kids. Most of my friends had children of different ages. I watched the children running after the clown, who was pretending to run away with the balloons.

"They bring life to a party, my mother-in-law always says," Vanessa said as she approached me.

"I have to agree. They have no worries in the world," I tried to be considerate and careful of what I said.

Dalton and Vanessa were married for five years. Their wedding was beautiful. The reception was at a golf club, just north of Toronto. The banquet room accommodated six hundred guests. Everything about their wedding was elegant. Dalton approached us, stood behind Vanessa, and rubbed her belly.

"Did you share our news with Cerise?" he asked.

"No, this is her day, not ours," she whispered and smiled at me.

"Does this mean you're...?" I began to say.

"Yes, we are pregnant!" Dalton said.

"I'm so happy for you both. How far along are you?"

"Fourteen weeks. We did not want to tell anyone until the first trimester was over," Vanessa was glowing with excitement.

"That's wonderful news!" I hugged both of them.

"What's wonderful news?" Carter asked as he approached and over-heard the tail end of our conversation.

"We are expecting a baby," Dalton told his brother. Carter gave him a big, manly hug and patted him on his back, then gave Vanessa a gentle hug and a kiss on her cheek.

"So when's the big day?" Carter asked. He put his arm around my back and pulled me in tight by my waist.

"Our due date is February 12," Vanessa answered.

"Have you told Mom and Dad, yet?" Carter asked.

"No, not yet! I think after the party, when everyone leaves, we'll tell them," Vanessa replied. "I'm sure they will be so excited."

"I know they will be. That's a given," Carter said. "I have to steal the birthday girl away. Mom is bringing out the birthday cake." He guided me over to one of the tables.

When Mrs. Blake brought out the cake, everyone started to sing 'Happy Birthday.' I was a little embarrassed. Carter stood beside me and held my hand. I looked around at everyone and felt so loved. These people were my family I picked myself. Many birthdays growing up, were some of my loneliest times in my life, after my Mom died. I always envied other children who had both parents to raise them.

"Make a wish!" Hannah jumped with excitement. She was standing right in front of the cake with her sister.

"Don't tell anyone, or else your wish won't come true." Savannah added.

I blew out the candles after making my wish. It was a beautiful cake. The cake was perfect with pink fondant icing and daisy flowers. It was so summery. The catering staff took over cutting the cake and handed it out to everyone, with coffee or tea.

"Now, time for birthday spanking," one of the little boys yelled out. He was the son of one of my friends from university. Everyone started to laugh. We could see Kyle, Dalton, and Preston in the back of the crowd, spanking each other, and each of them had a different facial expressions of pain, excitement or surprised looks.

"How about we save the spanking for later?" Carter told the little boy. He seemed happy with Carter's answer but was mostly amused that his comment, made everyone laugh. He stood there looking proud to be the center of attention.

"I will spank you privately, later." Carter whispered in my ear. I laughed and smacked his arm. He seemed happy, celebrating my birthday again. I gave him a kiss.

"Thank you, Carter, this party is special because of you." I smiled gently. "How long have you been planning this party?"

"Five weeks, this date worked for a couple of reasons. You would not suspect a thing having it after your birthday. Most people had vacation plans in August and I really wanted everyone here. This date worked for everyone," he explained. "I hope you were surprised."

"Yes, I was surprised. You thought of everything. I'm such a lucky girl to have you." I gave him a hug, which led to a kiss. "Why throw me a party? Going out to dinner on my birthday was perfect too."

"A few months ago, at the twins' birthday party, you made a comment that you did not have birthday parties as a child and you had so much fun, when I arranged your twenty-fifth surprise birthday party," he paused. "That was seven years ago. So I thought I should do it again." He smiled and held me tight against him.

It was true! I did not have parties for my birthday, when I was a child. Mom could not afford to do it. She would always make a homemade cake and had a little gift for me. She always made me feel special on my birthday. Sometimes she would take me to the park or go for a bike ride, but my favorite activity was going to the beach to spend the day swimming in the water.

"I hope you did not think I was hinting for another party."

"Weren't you?" Carter grinned.

Mrs. Blake approached us. She seemed to be having a great time with her three boys and entertaining my friends for the afternoon. She was the kind of person who liked to make people happy. Carter had the same character trait. "Sweetheart, everyone is excited to see you open your birthday gifts, especially the kids." She reached out for my hand. "Come on, I have a special chair for you to sit in."

"The party is enough. Gifts are too much." I looked at Carter and he shrugged his shoulders and smiled. I followed Mrs. Blake over to the chair. The children were in front of me, wanting me to open their gift first. It was so cute.

I started to open my gifts and before long I realized there was a theme. I received sundresses, bathing suits, a beach bag filled with sunscreen/towel/sun hat/flip-flops, dressy sandals, a manicure and pedicure gift certificate, and Mr. and Mrs. Blake gave me a complete luggage set. I was thrilled and over-whelmed. Everyone gave a gift relating to a summer theme. However, the luggage was questionable.

"One more gift!" Carter handed me an envelope. He smiled ear-to-ear.

I opened the envelope. Inside were two round trip tickets for a Caribbean cruise and the itinerary as well. I did not even have a chance to read the card. I saw Carter's name written on the bottom with many hugs and kisses. I jumped out of my seat and into Carter's arms, giving him a huge hug. He did not expect that reaction. He had to regain his balance, when I jumped on him. Everyone began to clap. Mrs. Blake, Sam, and Becky were crying. I began to cry too, in Carter's arms. I did not travel when I was a child. It was too expensive for our family. As an adult, I had the money but did not travel for a couple of reasons... First, I was focused on building my business and did not take time off. Second, I did not have someone to travel with. This was a dream come true.

"Are you happy?" he asked.

"Happy does not express how I feel. I am beyond happy. Thank you so much." I released my tight hug and he let me down. I patted my face with a tissue Savannah gave me.

I took a deep breath and faced my guests. "Thank you for coming. I love all of your gifts. You are too generous, and I am so lucky to have each one of you in my life. Thanks again, I was truly surprised."

Everyone kept this a secret for five weeks. How did I not figure it out? It was an amazing day. Before long, our guests, except for Carter's family, had left. Our guests had a wonderful time and the children enjoyed swimming in the pool and playing games.

"Carter, I can't believe we are going on a cruise." *I had to pinch myself, to make sure I was not dreaming.*

"Does that mean you're taking me with you?" Carter asked.

"If you're a good boy!"

"I know it's something you have dreamt about doing for a long time," he smiled. "I want to make your dreams and wishes come true."

"You have managed to make a few of my dreams come true already." I winked at him.

Chapter Fifteen

We drove home in Carter's Jeep. Ray followed us back to Carter's apartment. It was 7:00 p.m. I planned to go to bed earlier. I was excited to see my new office again. I had not been back since my private tour. It brought a smile to my face as I thought about my boardroom table and Carter between my legs.

Carter noticed me smiling. "What are you smiling about?" he asked.

"You make me happy." I put my hand on top of his, which was resting on the stick shift.

"The feeling is mutual," he smiled.

We were almost home. Carter and Ray grabbed the luggage and gifts from the car. I grabbed a few gift bags and held the doors for them as they entered the building. We had a great weekend and wonderful Sunday. I opened the apartment door, to let everyone in. Before I could step in, Ray yelled. "Get back." Carter dropped everything and pulled me towards him. Ray was in the apartment, searching each room. My heart pumped faster. From what I could see, the apartment did not look out of place. Something triggered Ray. Something was not right.

Ray returned with a disgusted look on his face. "The apartment is clear, but someone's been here," he paused and looked uncomfortable. "Miss Brooks I need to talk to Mr. Blake for a moment in private. Would you mind sitting on the sofa for a moment?" I nodded.

Carter and Ray were in the office for no more than a minute before Carter ran out towards his bedroom. I could hear him mutter something, which sounded like, "Fuck!" Then a door slammed. He stood in the hallway and took a deep breath before he approached me. He walked slowly and ran his fingers through his hair, with a worried look on his face.

"Carter, what's going on?" My voice and hands trembled.

Ray returned to Carter's office. I could not hear his conversation but I knew he was talking to Kyle.

Carter sat beside me on the sofa. He took my hands in his and rubbed them gently. He tried to find the words to tell me what happened. It was not like Carter to stumble on his words. He was a well-spoken man who had no difficulty with public speaking. Seeing this side of him was unsettling.

"What is it, Carter? You look like you've seen a ghost."

"This is difficult for me," he took a deep breath. "Someone was in my apartment today."

I looked around, confused. His apartment was not touched. Everything was still in place. Ray returned to the living room, with the same concerned expression, as Carter.

"Carter, you're scaring me. I'm confused."

"It's Lulu!"

"What about Lulu?" His eyes were sad. He looked down at the floor and nervously rubbed the palms of his hands, on his pants. "What's wrong with Lulu?" My voice began to quiver. *What was in the bedroom?* I stood up to go see for myself. Carter put his hand around my wrist when I stood up.

"Please don't go...I don't want you to see it," Carter pleaded.

I twisted my wrist out of Carter's grip and ran to the bedroom to search for Lulu. I opened the bathroom door. Tears began to run down my face. Lulu hung from the light fixture, with a rope around her neck. I screamed in horror. Carter was behind me, with his hands on my shoulders. I walked over to Lulu and touched her paws and tail. "Why?" I screamed with sadness.

"Cerise, I think we should go back out into the living room. Kyle will want this room untouched." Carter guided me out of the room. I was sobbing on the sofa when Kyle and Scott arrived. They were busy with their investigation, around Carter's apartment. Within thirty minutes, Carter's apartment was full of people who specialized in crime scenes. This was déjà vu. I was reliving the same emotions I had four days ago at my apartment. Except my precious Lulu was taken from me in a ruthless way.

I over heard Carter and Kyle talking. "The note said DIE in red lipstick." Kyle told him. I did not even notice the note attached to Lulu's collar. Everything else was a blur. "This is a death threat. We need to get security for both you and Cerise. We will put an officer outside your apartment too."

Carter analyzed the red lipstick messages in the order I received them. "BITCH. TO. NEEDS. DIE." he spoke aloud.

"BITCH NEEDS TO DIE." I spoke up. "I think I was supposed to find my apartment trashed before I received the black envelope at the restaurant. But I was not at my apartment because I stayed at Carter's." I blew my nose. "Whoever this is really wants me dead. I don't think they will stop until I am."

Carter and Kyle exchanged a look. "We're going to do everything we can to catch this person." Kyle tried to sooth me. Carter sat down beside me and I cuddled into his shoulder. I felt safe in his arms.

"How did Ray know something was not right?" I asked.

"There should have been a chime go off when the door opened. It did not go off." Carter explained.

"I thought the alarms were supposed to be a deterrent," I was confused.

"They are. This person seems to know their way around an alarm system."

"Then that means I am not safe anywhere," I blurted out.

"We are going to increase security and will upgrade the alarm system, as Ray suggested." Carter tried to console me.

"Maybe we should not stay here. Someone has been in here too! Who says they won't come back?" My paranoia was getting the better of me.

"This place is going to be the safest." Carter paused and looked at me. "Trust me, I'm not going to let you out of my sight."

"Why do you think this is happening? Do you still think Nicole would be capable of doing this?" I had so many unanswered questions.

"At this point, I don't know. At first, I thought so. I really don't know her well enough to judge," he answered honestly.

I walked to the bathroom across from the living room. I did not think I had any more tears to shed. I was numb. There was only one other time in my life I felt so depressed...that was when my mother was murdered. I felt disconnected from the world. I did not think I would be able to go into the en-suite bathroom, in Carter's bedroom again. I sat in the bathroom for a long time and sobbed. My face was swollen and red. Lulu was gone. How could anyone do this to my sweet and loving cat? I could not make sense of it.

"Cerise, you okay?" Carter asked through the locked bathroom door.

"Not really!" Carter started to jiggle the door handle. I immediately looked over.

"Sweetheart, please open the door. Let me help you."

I continued to look at the door. There was another hole underneath the door handle. *Strange! Was that normal?* I saw it in my apartment as well. I crawled over to the door and looked out the peephole. I could see Carter pacing in front of the door. I had a clear view of the living room when Carter walked to either side of the hole. Carter stopped in front of the door and knocked. It startled me. I fell back onto the floor.

"Cerise, please open the door. I do not want to force my way in." Carter said firmly. I struggled to open the door slipping on the tile. I opened the door and jumped into Carter's arms.

"Carter, I'm scared." I started to cry and ramble hysterically, but nobody could understand what I was saying.

"It's okay. Come sit down. Let's breathe and slow down." Carter remained calm. He took me over to the sofa where I sat before. He made me take a few deep breaths. It helped me calm down slightly.

"Let's start over. What happened in the bathroom?" Carter asked. He sat beside me on the sofa, holding my hand. Kyle was kneeling on the floor, in front of me and Scott was standing behind Kyle.

"Is it normal to have holes under the door handles?" I asked. I was not a carpenter or interior designer. I assumed it was not, but I needed them to answer the question.

Carter, Kyle, and Scott looked over at the door handle. From the living room, it looked like a black dot. Scott walked over to investigate further. Then he walked around to the other doors in the apartment.

"All the doors have them. There is wood shaving on the floor by each door. They were freshly drilled." Scott informed everyone.

"I noticed it at my apartment the other day too," I recalled. "I thought it was odd too. I was so upset, I did not think anything of it, until now." I paused "This is hard for me to say, as it brings back difficult memories of my childhood." I took a deep breath. Everyone was silent and listening to each word. "Tony, my mom's boyfriend, drilled holes in all the doors in our townhouse, to watch me get dressed or undress, in rooms I thought were private areas." I began to cry. "I don't know if it's a coincidence, but why are there holes under the handles, like he made sixteen years ago?" Carter rubbed my back gently and passed me a tissue. Carter, Kyle, and Scott exchanged looks.

"Cerise, if I recall, Tony Russo received a life sentence of twenty-five years in jail, with a chance of parole after fifteen years, for Second-degree murder," he paused. "Is that correct?"

"Yes, he's in jail." Tears ran down my face.

"I'm going to look into this further. I'm sure you would be on the list of names to notify if he were up for a parole hearing or release," he patting me on the shoulder. Kyle and Scott left us alone and talked privately in Carter's office. I could hear them making phone calls to inquire about Tony Russo.

"Cerise, can I get you a bottle of water? Tylenol? Anything?" Carter asked.

"Water and Tylenol would be great. My head is pounding."

Carter walked to the kitchen and returned with a water bottle and Tylenol. I took it immediately. He grabbed a blanket and made me comfortable on the sofa. He left me when Kyle called him over. They were deep in conversation. The apartment was still full of people wandering around me. By the time everyone left, it was close to midnight, except for Ray, Phillip, Kyle, and Scott. They instructed us to get some sleep and they would know more the following day. *How could I sleep in the apartment, with everything that happened?* They had undercover officers watching our apartment outside the building and another officer outside our door. Ray and Phillip were guarding the inside. They were going to take shifts. Carter would be by my side through the night. I should have felt safe having extra protection, but I was not convinced.

I knew in my heart it was Tony's doing. He wanted me dead. When found guilty of second-degree murder, sixteen years ago, he yelled in the courtroom, "You will pay with your life for this, BITCH!"

Chapter Sixteen

I still had the vision of Lulu hanging from the light fixture, fresh in my mind. There was no other choice but to use the bathroom to shower. I cried the entire time. I dressed in my black skinny jeans, my black tank top and pulled on my black riding boots. I did not realize how tired I looked until I seen my reflection in the mirror. I grabbed my black leather jacket and walked to the living room. Everyone greeted me. Carter walked over to me and gave me a gentle kiss. "Maybe we should stay home today and rest," he suggested.

"No, I need to be at the office today. The moving company will be there before noon." I gave him a forced smile. "Besides, I don't want to let this person ruin my life. I need to focus and continue with my daily schedule."

"Okay, I understand. I have increased the security. I hired three more security personnel. Ray is in charge. There will be two security guards with you, always. They will be working twelve-hour shifts opposite each other. Unfortunately, you won't be able to go to the bathroom without it being inspected first," he advised. "It is temporary until the culprit is caught."

"No objection," I agreed. "Do you have any information regarding Tony? Is he still in jail?"

"No news yet. Kyle called about thirty minutes ago, and he said he'd meet us at your office in an hour," he glanced at his watch. "I want you to eat something, then we will head over there."

"I'm not hungry," I replied.

"You did not even eat dinner last night, so I want you to eat."

He took a few phone calls in his office while I ate. Ray sat across from me and read the newspaper.

"Ray, have you ever been in a situation like this before?" I asked.

"Yes, many times. Unfortunately, this is the reason I'm usually hired." His facial features were gentle but concerned.

"So what is the outcome?"

"Typically the criminal is caught and sentenced. Time is the question. Sometimes it happens quickly and other times they are smart and harder to catch." He paused and looked directly into my eyes. "In most cases the victim is always protected. Please let me do the worrying." he smiled sincerely.

Everywhere I looked reminded me of Lulu. Her food and water bowls, her favorite spot on the sofa, and her toys that were scattered around on the floor, were all triggers of sadness. I really missed her rubbing my legs in a figure eight pattern and her impatient meows when she waited for her breakfast. I tried hard to control my emotions but it was difficult.

We gathered up our belongings and were escorted to Ray's vehicle. Carter and I sat in the rear seat together. Ray and Phillip sat in the front.

"We will meet everyone at your office, this morning. Everyone will be cleared out before the moving company arrives," he explained.

"Who's going to protect you?" I asked.

"Phillip will be with me always. He has a black belt in Jujitsu. I think I'm protected," he smiled. I was worried about him because everyone I have ever loved left me. I did not want anything to happen to Carter.

We arrived at my office to find the boardroom full of people. They were waiting on us to arrive. As soon as we entered, Kyle introduced us to everyone in the room. Mr. Blake was present as well. He was involved with the Tony Russo case, sixteen years ago. He wanted to be there to help the investigation in any way he could.

"The purpose of today's meeting is to discuss what we already know and what our action plan is, to catch Tony Russo," Kyle began.

"So we know it is Tony." I interrupted.

"Yes, he is our main suspect. He was released on parole, three months ago. He is in a halfway house in Scarborough. We have people watching every move he makes. He has been home for his curfew each night. This is why the acts have happened during the day. He is able to leave during the day for work but has to return home by 7:00 p.m. each day. Right now we can't prove anything," he paused and looked at me. "We will catch him, Cerise."

"We will take the necessary precautions to keep you safe," Scott added.

"Why wasn't Cerise notified, he was released? Or even up for parole?" Carter asked.

"We're investigating that. Cerise should have been on the computer records. However, her name is not on file. Her name was documented on the filed hardcopy, only. We are investigating to find out, if it was a human data entry error, or deleted after the fact. During Tony's prison time, he studied computer programming. We are investigating this as well," he reported.

"This may be an odd question, but why are we meeting here in my office instead of the police station?"

"We thought we should meet here, in case he is watching you. If he saw you in the police station, he might get scared off. We do not want to scare him off. We wore suits and drove unmarked vehicles here, for that reason. He would not recognize us, as we could be employees who work in this building. He is a smart man. I'm sure he knows Carter's schedule, not to mention he is probably familiar with the details of vehicles you drive, friends, place you go often...not just you but of those who are with you the most, which includes Ray and Phillip," he stated. "He knows he has stirred the pot, but he does not know we, or I should say, you, made the connection of the clue he left behind. He knew only you would recognize those holes and make the personal connection. Therefore, our goal is to continue with our lives, as normal as possible. This time we will see him coming and not the other way around."

"My life is upside down, right now. There is nothing normal about this."

"We understand. Please trust us." Kyle patted me on my shoulders.

Kyle and Scott continued to give instructions to everyone in the boardroom. He briefed every one on Tony Russo's history. Everyone at the meeting had classified folders that contained information about Tony. They were confident they were going to be there, when Tony messed up, but I knew it would not be easy. He was a heartless excuse for a human being. Now he wanted revenge on me.

I was angry. I wanted revenge too. I wanted him to pay for taking my mom and Lulu away from me.

Everyone left around 11:30 a.m. I expected the moving company to come by noon. I felt the sudden urgency to contact Mrs. Rosh. We had our follow-up appointment scheduled in a week. I really did not want to wait until next Monday to finish my Will. I thought hard about whom I wanted my beneficiary to be, so I decided to call her before the moving company arrived. Carter was busy with the security personnel.

"Hello, Mrs. Rosh. Do you have a few minutes?" I spoke into the phone.

"Yes, how may I help you today?" she asked.

"I would like to get my Will finished, ASAP. I know you are waiting on some information from me. Could I give you the information now?"

"Yes, of course, let me grab your file." She put me on hold briefly. "Your Will is almost complete. We were waiting on how you want to divide your estate. How many beneficiaries would you like to put on your Will?" she asked.

"It was not hard to decide. I have not prepared a Will before but I have worked it out as a percentage instead of a dollar amount, as my investments can increase substantially in a short time. I would like my friends Rebecca, Samantha and Kyle to receive ten per cent, Savannah and Hannah five per cent in a Trust fund, ten per cent to the MC Foundation for Abused Women and Children, and the remaining fifty percent to Carter Blake"

She recorded my request. She took everyone's full names and other details. She did not question or persuade my decisions. She gave me the information and let me make my own decision after receiving her professional advice. I loved that about her.

"Thank you for calling me. I will complete your will and have it ready to sign first thing tomorrow morning," she advised.

"Thank you. I will come by tomorrow morning. Thanks again for your help."

I felt much better having the Will, off my mind. I was usually optimistic, but under the circumstances, I felt I was being realistic.

Carter knocked on my office door with a sandwich and an iced tea in his hands. "Lunch? I thought you'd be hungry."

"Thank you. I am hungry. I think I can eat a horse." I laughed.

Carter leaned over the desk to give me a kiss.

"You know where kisses lead us. We better not go there, the moving company should be here any moment."

"I'm sure we could manage a quickie," he joked with arched eyebrows.

He sat down on the other side of my desk and we ate our lunch together. We talked about everything but Tony Russo. Carter knew me so well. He was a pro at changing my mind and distracting me.

"I think you should get back to work. I'm sure the boss is not happy about you not showing up to work today," I teased. Being a Senior Partner at the firm had its benefits.

"I have an understanding boss," he teased back. "However, I will have to go to my office after lunch. I have a client meeting, which I cannot miss. Do you think you'll be okay here without me for a few hours?"

"Yeah, I will be fine. Once the moving company gets here I will have plenty to do to keep my mind occupied," I answered honestly.

"Ray is talking to the new security staff. He will introduce you to them after lunch. Ray will be going home to sleep and return later for the next shift. You will have two security guards here. I programmed your phone to speed dial me should anything happen. If you do not feel comfortable about something, call me. Here, let me show you how it works." He took my phone and he showed me how to use the speed dial.

Ray knocked on the door. Carter asked them to come in. There were three men standing with Ray, in my office. They were big and muscular. They were equipped with earpieces to communicate to each other. They had special training on the police force and undercover surveillance work.

"Cerise, I want to introduce you to these men who will be working with me. This is Jagger, Max, and Stone." They reached out and shook my hand. "They have my direct line should they need backup. The two off-duty staff will always be on call. The first shift will be Jagger and Max. They will assist you in any way possible. Please communicate with them when you need to go somewhere. They will gladly escort you." Ray was kind. I have grown to really trust and respect him. He explained their shifts would be twelve hours long, switching at 6 p.m. and 6 a.m. Therefore, Ray and Stone were going to return in six hours for their first shift, to be on schedule.

Ray and Stone left the office shortly there after. Jagger and Max started with a six-hour shift. Like Ray, they were detailed oriented. They inspected the building, halls, bathrooms, etc. One of them was always with me, not hovering over me, but close enough. It was something I had to get used to.

The moving company arrived, right on time. Jagger and Max checked them out before they were able to start moving the boxes into my office. I think they were surprised to have two large, muscular men supervising them. They were efficient and had the boxes moved into the designated office space within an hour and a half. There was no office furniture to move, as Carter arranged for me to keep the existing furniture in the office. The moving part was easy. The challenge was to unpack and arrange the files in the filing cabinets. This was what would take the most time. I was still excited to be in my new office, but the stress of Tony Russo was still in the back of my mind.

I kept revisiting my memories of the night my mother was murdered in my head. I still felt the fear, I felt that night...

My mother did not want Tony to touch me again. That started the fight that dreadful night. Earlier in the evening, I had been washing the dishes at the counter, when Tony made a comment that he wanted me to wash the dishes naked, for him. He then laughed, to make it appear he was joking. It was uncomfortable and I could not concentrate on washing the dishes, with him watching me. He sat at the table behind me. My mom was not home yet. She worked in a retail store and worked different shifts. I expected her within thirty minutes.

I heard him unzip his pants, moan slightly and I heard him spit. I assumed he spit on his hands for lubrication. I did not intend to turn around to see what he was doing. I knew! I was still a virgin, but at sixteen, you know. I heard the moist noise of his hand rubbing against his penis. I heard the kitchen chair creaking. I could barely continue the dishes. I was afraid to turn and confront him, in fear of what he would do to me. I was also afraid to stay and try to ignore him. I wanted my mother to come home. I was so deep in thought I did not realize he stood up and was standing behind me. I remember him saying in my ear, "I want your mouth on my cock." I jumped out of my skin.

I turned and said, "Fuck you."

He replied, "That's even a better idea." I ran out of the kitchen. He grabbed me and I fell to the ground. He put his hand up my skirt, while holding me with the other hand. He was so strong. I could not free myself. He tore my underwear off and started to touch me between my legs. I struggled, squeezed my legs together, and fought until I exhausted myself. I really did not want to lose my virginity that way. I cried out for help. My mother came through the door, heard my cries, and ran to the kitchen to find Tony half naked with a hard-on and me crying on the floor, with his hand up my skirt. His focus was on me. He did not see or hear my mother enter the room. My mom kicked him in the face with her high heel shoes. It knocked him off me, onto the ground.

I immediately jumped up and ran to my room. I could hear Tony trying to smooth everything over with my mom. It seemed like it was working. Everything seemed calm. An hour passed by. Then I heard the doorbell. I forgot I arranged to have Rebecca sleep over that night. After what happened, I wanted to sleep at her house instead. My mom sent her up to my room. I remember telling Rebecca everything in detail. I cried a lot.

We put a movie on and opened up our snacks, which I had already organized earlier in the day. We did not watch the movie. I was busy making plans to run away. I could not live there anymore. I did not know where I would go, but I knew I could not stay. It was about two hours later when my mother and Tony started to fight again, over me. He had been drinking for two hours straight. Their verbal arguing turned into a physical fight. Rebecca and I could hear all the struggles and furniture breaking from upstairs. When I ran downstairs to help my mom, Rebecca called the police. I could not help my mom. I was too late. He had strangled her. He yelled at her motionless body and called her names. He sat on her stomach with his hands still around her neck. I felt so helpless. It seemed like everything was in slow motion. Rebecca grabbed my arm, which jolted me back to reality. She pulled on my arm forcefully in the direction of the front door, to run out of the house...

I tried my hardest to keep these horrible memories out of my head. I managed to keep myself busy unpacking files. I also arranged my desk space and hooked up my computer and printer. I was now able to work in my office. Arranging the files would probably take a couple more days to complete. Time slipped by. It was 6 p.m. Carter showed up in my office, leaning against the doorframe with a sexy smile. "You look 'hot' behind your new desk, Miss Brooks," he observed.

"Thank you. The furniture has that affect on me," I joked.

"The furniture has nothing to do with it." He approached my desk and sat on the edge. "I missed you today," He gave me a kiss on my lips.

"I missed you too."

"Will you be ready to go home soon?" He paused and looked at his watch. "Ray and Stone are here for the shift switch," he told me.

"Yes, I have to turn off my computer and lock the cabinets and I'm ready."

"I will meet you out front." He left my office, turning once to wink at me.

Moments later, I joined Carter. By the look on his face, he was not happy. His mood had changed from moments earlier, in my office. He was holding a vase with a dozen red roses, obviously not from him. His mood would be more pleasant if they were.

"These were delivered." He handed them to me. I put the vase on the receptionist desk and read the card. It read ~ *I hope your new office is as special as you are! Alec xo*

"Am I reading too deep into this? Do you have something to tell me?" Carter was angry. Over the years, I have seen him get angry only a handful of times. He usually did not overreact. He was confident and was not jealous of anyone or anything.

"Carter, I'm sure this is nothing more than a friendly welcoming bouquet. There's nothing to read into."

"I've known Alec since I was a child. This is not 'nothing'. Either you're naive or you're not telling me something."

"If you are insinuating that I am cheating, then you do not know me very well. I would not cheat. It is against everything I believe in. As far as I'm concerned, he is an arrogant jerk who thinks money can buy him everything." I defended myself. "I really can't wait for this merger contract to be over, so I don't ever have to deal with him again."

"I know who you are. I know you would not cheat on me...but that does not stop Alec from trying. I don't trust him." He ran his fingers through his hair in frustration. "So you can honestly say he hasn't come on to you."

"Maybe these flowers are for you," I said sarcastically. "Maybe he wants you to think something is going on, to get a reaction from you. You both seem to have an equal hatred towards one another, which I still, don't understand."

"Maybe you're right. I wouldn't put it past him to do something like this." He walked over to me and closed the gap between us. He stared into my eyes searching for the truth. Being a lawyer, he has developed a skill of reading someone without a lie-detector test. "You didn't answer my question. Has he come on to you?"

"Yes, he has!" I confessed. I could not lie to him. He would know.

"I knew it. My instincts were telling me this, since I saw him at the gala." He turned and paced the waiting room back and forth. "First the dance club, then the Gala, then he turns out to be the merger partner you're working for, now this? What's next?"

"I handled it. I told him I would walk away from this merger if he was unprofessional."

"So I guess this is a professional gesture with kisses and hugs on the card. I don't think he received the message loud and clear from you." His words hurt. It was true. Alec was being unprofessional.

"Everything you've said is true." I looked over at the beautiful flowers. I was feeling overwhelmed with emotion. Everything I had with Carter was wonderful. Alec was building a wall between us. I had to put a stop to it. I knew in my heart that I had to walk away from the merger. That would eliminate any connection with Alec. "I'll walk away from the merger." I exhaled a deep breath. My heart hurt as I said the words. I have worked hard to have an opportunity like this.

"Cerise, lets not make drastic decisions." He walked back over to me and looked into my eyes once again. "I know how important this is for you. Maybe it will not be so bad, since you are in your own office. You won't see him on a daily basis." I think he was trying to convince himself, as he said the words to me.

"Carter, you knew how I felt about turning our friendship into a relationship. My worst fear was losing my best friend. Now my worst fear is losing what we have together because of this merger. Please don't let Alec have that much power."

"He will not have that much power over us."

"Carter you really have to tell me why you dislike each other."

"I'll tell you everything over dinner."

Chapter Seventeen

Neither of us wanted to cook. I was tired, emotionally and physically. We picked up Chinese food on the way back to Carter's apartment. I loved the Chinese takeout restaurant we went to, not only for the great food, but because they used the traditional Chinese takeout boxes. Carter opened a bottle of wine and poured us both a glass. Instead of eating at the table, we ate on the sofa in front of the fireplace. We sat at opposite sides of the sofa, facing each other. I pulled the throw blanket over our legs.

"So tell me everything." I took a bite of my egg roll.

"Where do I begin?" He took a sip of his wine. "It began back in fifth grade. Alec was not popular and had been at my school for about six months. My mom met Alec's mother, at a SCC meeting at the school. Alec's mother told my mom; Alec was having difficulties socially. He was not doing well academically because of it. Of course, my mom, being who she is, wanted to help Alec. She asked me to be friends with him and get him involved in school activities. Therefore, I did. We became good friends. We hung out, played sports together, and before long, he was one of the gang. Many of my friends did not like him at first but tolerated him. Maybe out of pity or because they knew I had his back." He paused and made eye contact with me. "Everyone always compared him to me. I hated it. His mom would say, 'Why can't you get good grades like Carter?' or 'Try to workout more like Carter, so you can be on the football team.' The list was long. Then when it was time for high school, we both attended a private school, for the first semester together. I hated it there. I needed a balance of sports and academics to keep me interested in school, so I transferred to the public high school. Alec stayed at the private school. His mother would not allow him to transfer schools. She felt the private school offered a better education. He was unhappy there. Once I left, his social life died. Most of my friends stopped hanging out with him because he was always trying to prove he was better than everyone. We did not see much of each other after switching schools. My high school years were with you, Kyle, Sam, and Becky."

"Sounds like a terrible childhood for him."

"It wasn't all bad. He had everything a child needed and more. He had the latest games and motorized toys, on the market. We both came from wealthy families but grew up very different. My father refused to spoil us with material things. So it was cool hanging out with Alec because he had the fun toys." He paused and ate some of his Chinese food. "We would see each other a few times each year through social functions our parents took us to. At those functions, his mother would brag about my successes—not Alec's. She would talk about my awards, or what a coach said, about my sports abilities. I personally did not hear this myself but other people told me. To make a long story short, he was always trying to have the upper hand. We did not have any hatred towards each other back then."

"That's so sad but explains a lot."

"We met up in law school. The first year we hung out and studied together. It was like old times. Until..." Carter paused and was deep in thought.

"Until, what?"

"I was dating a girl who was studying law, as well. Her name was Jenna. I am not sure if you remember her. You may have met her a couple of times." Carter looked at me before continuing. "Alec had developed an obsession with Jenna. It was his personal revenge on me. He spent his time trying to impress Jenna. I found out later that he often bought her gifts. By the way, it started with a dozen red roses." He looked at me to see my reaction. I frowned and waited for him to continue. "He won her over with his wealth and slick ways. She found him attractive and liked how he showered her with attention and gifts."

"I had no idea."

"Alec and I shared an apartment off campus. One night I came home from a study group I was apart of and caught them in bed together. My bed! She was the first person I had developed feeling for, since high school. Alec and I had huge fistfight. He ended up in the hospital with a broken nose. Jenna told me she would not do it again, but it was too late for repair... I could not trust her again. It was over."

"That explains why you have not had a serious relationship."

"This is why I don't trust him. He's a snake."

"I'm not Jenna. I would not let him come between us." I moved closer to him and snuggled into his side. "My heart belongs to you." I

118

kissed him gently. I could tell he was still upset. He did not kiss me back passionately, as he usually did.

Carter's phone rang and interrupted our conversation. He decided to take the call in his office. I waited for him to return but he seemed to be distracted with details relating to a court case. I knocked on the door before entering. "Carter?" I whispered.

I heard him talking on the phone, "I have told you already. Stay away from her or I will get a restraining order against you." He turned to see who was at the door. His face lit up and waved me to come in. "Are we clear?" he asked firmly. "Good." He hung up the phone.

"Sounds like trouble." I sat in one of his guest chairs.

"Nothing for you to worry about," he said with a crooked smile.

"I have only been in your home office once and it was only for a minute, so I did not have a chance to look around. It's beautiful in here." His office had modern furniture like the rest of his apartment. However, it had an art gallery feeling. In his apartment, he had famous artist's paintings throughout on display. In his office, it was his personal paintings displayed everywhere. The first portrait he painted of me in art class hung over the gas fireplace. I loved that portrait. "You still have this portrait of me? Wow, that was a long time ago." I stood up to go look at the other paintings he had done. I recognized a few because of the awards he won. Most of them were new to me. "You're an incredible artist."

"Thank you. I still paint and sketch sometimes. I find it relaxing." He was right behind me and put his hands around my waist to hug me. "I'm glad you like them. You're my inspiration." He kissed my neck.

"I am?" I tilted my head to the side, to allow him to kiss more of my neck.

"My paintings or sketches are inspired by your beauty." He stopped kissing me. He took my hand and walked over to a painting with a view of the lake, from the deck at his cottage. I recognized it, as it was my favorite view. "Do you recognize this view? This is where I would find you in the morning with your tea, whenever you came to the cottage. A few years ago, I wanted to capture the view through your eyes. So I sat in your spot and painted this picture," he explained.

"It is beautiful. No words can express its beauty."

Then he walked over to another painting. "This was inspired by our camping weekend on Canada Day long weekend, ten years ago. Everyone was partying at our campsite. We decided to take a walk.

We were cozy against each other, lying on the beach. The dark sky was so clear. Do you remember that night? I was hypnotized by the bright stars."

"Yes, I remember it as if it were yesterday. We talked for a long time about our dreams and desires. It was a beautiful night."

"Well, this picture captures that moment with you." We both stared at his painting. It was a painting of the lake, with the moon's reflection and multitude of stars in the sky. The water was so calm and each ripple had a sparkle.

"You're such a romantic. Do you have a picture of what happened after?" I asked.

"Not on canvas," he smiled at me with his sexy look. "That picture is for my eyes only."

"What do you remember?" I asked.

"I remember we kissed. It was perfect under the stars. Everyone decided to join us on the beach. The girls wanted to go skinny-dipping. I did not want to because I had a hard-on from kissing you," he laughed as he remembered the details. "Sam and Becky grabbed your hand and started running towards the water, pealing off your clothes, as well as their own. Then you were in the water, after I had a glance at your silhouette against the moon's reflection off the water." he smiled gently. "Did I leave out any details?"

"A couple, you did not leave me out there, for long. You, Kyle and Troy started to take off your clothes and joined us in the water. I remember seeing your rock hard body, too. I was a little shy. You swam to me and told me you had to come in to make sure I was safe because I had been drinking. I remember our naked bodies hugging each other. I did not want to touch the bottom of the lake. I was scared of the fish swimming in the lake that I could not see, so you held me safely in your arms." I laughed at the thought of it. "You were such a gentleman. You did not try to touch me inappropriately."

"We have to stop talking about this. I am hard and horny. I want to go skinny dipping with you again." He kissed me passionately. My Carter was back.

"Me too," I admitted. "I love your paintings. Do you have any recent paintings or sketches?"

"I have a couple."

"Can I see them?"

"I'm still working on the final touches." He took my hand again and we walked over to a sliding door. He slid it open. There it was. It was the most realistic painting I have ever seen. It looked like a photo. It was the night of the Gala. He was in his tuxedo and I was in my black floor length dress. We were dancing. I was laughing at something Carter was saying to me. We looked happy together.

"Carter this is magnificent!" I was awe struck at his talent.

"It was our first dance as a couple," he admitted.

"You are the best thing that has ever happened to me." I put my arms around him and kissed him. He held me tight and kissed me back. "I can imagine the portraits you will do of our wedding." Oops, I said that aloud.

"There you go again. Are you asking me to marry you?" he asked teasingly.

We both laughed and continued to kiss each other.

Chapter Eighteen

My first week in my new office passed quickly. I had the merger files transferred over to my office, on Tuesday. I was able to focus on the merger without interruption and felt at ease in my own environment. It was working out so much better. I did not have any correspondence with Alec during the week, aside from the flowers, which came on Monday. If I had a question, his financial managers helped answer them.

Carter and I had lunch with each other every day. He seemed to be more at ease knowing Alec was not interacting with me daily. We spoke about what Alec had done and said to me. I felt so much better, with everything communicated. I no longer needed to hide information, so Carter would not get upset. He was much more understanding than I thought he would be. He had one request. He did not want me to be alone with Alec. I could live with that. I did not intend to put myself in that position again.

There had not been any other leads or clues to bring us closer to finding the person responsible for the notes, break-ins, or killing my precious Lulu. With the increased security this week, it was difficult for anyone to approach me. Meetings and deliveries had to go through my security team first.

We decided to spend the long weekend on Carter's new yacht. We talked about canceling our plans for this weekend, but after discussing it, we felt it was what we needed. We planned for our friends to come Saturday afternoon and stay the night. I was looking forward to seeing them again. We stopped by the yacht, stocked the fridge with food, beer, wine, and unpacked our clothes. I was excited to go back to the yacht. It was the first time sleeping there, and my first time sleeping on a boat, ever.

I thought about how the last two weeks with Carter, had been wonderful, despite the turmoil of my business and my unknown stalker. So much had happened in such a short time. Even with the negative, I was happy. I melted when Carter looked at me or touched me. His protective, caring ways made me fall in love with him even more.

Ray and Stone had switched shifts at 6:00 p.m. They had done their check of the office and surrounding area. We waited by the receptionist desk for Carter. As soon as I heard the elevator's bell ring, I knew it was Carter. He embraced me and gave me a kiss. We locked my office and left the building. We drove in Ray's SUV. It seemed to be the car of choice the past week.

Our evening on the yacht was romantic. The view of the water glistened, as the waves rolled towards the shore. It was magical. I brought my LED candles to give it a perfect ambiance. Carter poured us a glass of wine, and we sat on the main deck and talked about our week. He started to massage my feet. It did not take long before we finished the whole bottle of wine.

"Come on, I want to rock the boat." He took my hand and led me to the bedroom. We updated the bedroom with brand new linen on the bed. It looked so comfortable with the fluffy down-filled duvet. Everything matched perfectly. The duvet cover was navy and the sheets were white with a navy nautical design on it. We added extra throw pillows to finish the look.

"What about Ray and Stone? Won't they hear us?" I wondered.

"No, they won't. It is sound proof. Unless you start yelling God's name," he joked.

He closed the door and the window blinds. He dimmed the lights slightly. When he was done, he came over to me, pulled me in for a hug, and kissed me gently on my lips. We peeled each other's clothes off. He lowered me onto the bed.

"You are so beautiful." He kissed my breasts, and then he worked his way south and kissed every inch of me. I watched him kiss and lick my sensitive spot. We made eye contact several times. He loved making me come. He watched my reaction each time he moved his tongue over my sensitive spot. It would make me shiver and shake.

"You better stop or I'm going to start yelling God's name."

"I'd prefer it if you start yelling my name."

He rubbed my opening with his fingers before entering them. He stopped and positioned himself with his knees under my thighs. He rubbed the head of his cock against my clit. He smiled devilishly before he penetrated deep inside of me, with one thrust of his hips. I moaned loudly. I watched the muscles in his arms tighten with each push. "You're so hot and tight." He continued to push his cock into me with a steady rhythm. He stopped with his cock still inside of me and rolled us over so I was on top.

I kissed his neck and ran my hands through his hair. He smelled so good. I let his length slide out of me, while I balanced myself in a squatting position over him. Once he was inside of me, I started to move slowly, and then increased my speed with a steady rhythm. I felt him tensing and flexing his leg muscles to remain in control of his orgasm, which was near. "Slow down, Ma Cerise, I'm gonna come." I did not listen. I continued my fast speed until he came. I lay down beside him, my leg muscles still throbbed from the work out I had had.

"You're a wild girl in bed." He kissed the tip of my nose.

We waited for our guests to arrive on Saturday. We expected them around 1:00 p.m. We were excited to entertain our friends, on our new yacht. We heard a motorcycle in a distance. When we looked towards the marina's parking lot, we noticed it was Becky and Mike. Carter and I walked over to greet them in the parking lot. Carter was wearing his swimming trunks and a tee shirt with his loafers. I was wearing my black bikini, with a sheer black cover-up and my flip-flops. Carter had bought it for me during week.

I gave Becky a big hug. Carter shook Mike's hand. Carter and Mike instantly started to talk about Mike's bike. Becky looked incredibly sexy in her leather pants and leather jacket. She took off her leather jacket to reveal her bikini top. It was a mix of yellows and peachy oranges.

"Cerise!" I heard someone calling my name. I turned around to see Sam running our way. We greeted her with a hug. She was in her bikini too, with a cover-up. Carter greeted Kyle with a handshake and hugged him with the opposite arm, as they patted each other's back roughly.

"Nice bike. Becky lets get some pictures of you on it." Sam suggested.

Becky hopped on the bike. She started to pose in different ways as Sam took pictures, with her camera.

"Sam it's your turn," Becky grabbed Sam's camera.

"No, it's ok." She tried to refuse.

124

"Come on. You're gorgeous." Becky was helping her take off her cover-up. Sam sat on the bike with caution. She started to smile awkwardly and tried to pose as Becky did. She really was a natural beauty. She did not know it.

"Cerise, it's your turn," Becky sang. Carter was intrigued at this point and smiling ear-to-ear. Becky gave the camera back to Sam.

"I will probably fall off the bike and end up in the hospital."

"Don't be silly. Hop on." I hopped on the bike with caution like the way Sam did. It was my first time on a motorcycle. I smiled at Carter. Sam took pictures. His arms were crossed and his eyes were fixated on me. He stared at me with desire. So I assumed he liked what he saw.

"Wait a second. You have to take off your cover-up." Becky started to peel it off. I kicked off my flip-flops too. She made me giggle with embarrassment. She had no sense of shyness when it came to her body. She was used to people dressing her when she acted or modeled. I was inexperienced and private when it came to my body.

"Sit on the seat backwards, lean back so your head is resting here at the handles. Bend this leg like this, and stretch this leg here. Now arch your back and look at the sky. Excellent!" She instructed. I did as she told me.

"Okay, that's enough of my modeling. I'm surprised the camera did not break."

"You should be a model. You have the body, and you're really photogenic." Becky complimented.

"That's crazy, you watch, those pictures will be awkward looking," I replied.

"Okay we will see," she paused. "One more picture, but with Carter. Please," she begged.

She did not have to ask Carter twice. He took off his tee shirt and exposed his muscular chest and six-pack. He sat on the bike first and then helped me get on the bike. I faced him and held him tightly for balance. "Ride me baby." Everyone laughed. He held my waist to support and balance me, while I shifted my body into place. I bent my legs and put them around Carter. I arched my back and let my head drop back. A gust of warm wind blew by, blowing my hair around. I felt Carter's hard cock through my bikini. He bent down and kissed between my breasts.

"Okay, bad boy, I think thats enough fun for one day," I slapped his arm. "People are watching." I hopped off the bike and stood beside

Becky. Carter stood behind me, and hugged me around my waist. I did not know how many pictures Sam took, but I was interested to see how they turned out.

He whispered in my ear so no one else could hear him, "You drive me crazy." His voice gave me goose bumps.

"Come on, Sam," Kyle took Sam by the hand and guided her to the motorcycle. Becky took the camera from Sam and started to take pictures of them. He sat on the bike on the side instead of straddling it. He pulled Sam in tight. Sam's legs were wide and showing off her butt.

"Look over your shoulder, Sam," Becky instructed. Becky had some great shots.

"It's your turn, Becky." I took the camera away from her. Both Becky and Mike were wearing leather pants. Mike took off his shirt and exposed his buff upper body. Becky was still in her bikini top and leather pants. They both sat together on the bike, both facing the front. The warm air picked up again and swirled Becky's hair around, making it look like they were really driving the bike. It was amazing.

"Who knew my bike would get this attention today?" Mike laughed. Kyle and Carter agreed. They continued to talk more about his bike. Carter and Kyle seemed interested in buying one. I put on my cover-up before grabbing someone's overnight bag to bring to the yacht. We were attracting some attention from people passing by. Becky was used to this attention, but it made me self-conscience and a little uncomfortable. I was excited to show our friends our yacht. I encouraged everyone to follow Carter.

"Shall we go?" I asked everyone. "I have my computer. We can download those pictures onto it." I smiled. Everyone grabbed their belongings and followed Carter.

We passed a group of people in the parking lot. They were in there twenties. One of the guys blurted boldly, "Hey, Blondie, you're looking HOT. Can I take you to dinner?" It was obvious the question was meant for me, as I was the only blond girl.

Carter stopped in his tracks, thought before he spoke, as he always did. I knew Carter was not a fighter, but he had a look in his eyes, which made me think he might. Instead, he made a joke out of it and said, "Sorry! I am not available. I'm flattered you asked." Everyone started to laugh, including the twenty year olds, except for the person who made the comment.

His friends hit his arm and laughed. "Awe, too bad! It's not like you ever had a chance." We continued to walk.

Kyle was the last one, in our line formation. He flashed his badge. "Don't start any trouble. Move along!" The guys continued in the opposite direction from the parking lot.

We arrived at our yacht. Our friends were so impressed and loved it, as much, as we did. We offered everyone drinks and had a toast to friendship. It was a beautiful, sunny day. There was not a cloud to be seen anywhere. We enjoyed our time together. Carter suggested we go out on the lake. We toured the Toronto Harbourfront and Islands. Later, Carter took us to Woodbine Beach. We stayed a distance from the busy beach, but it was still close enough to swim to shore if we wanted to. Becky, Sam, and I sun tanned on the nose of the yacht. Carter, Kyle, and Mike swam.

Carter played music from his iPod wirelessly to his speaker system. The music he chose was his cottage playlist of old classic rock songs. The songs were about summer, having fun, and parties. We had a wonderful day in the sun, like the old days.

We decided to go out to dinner to a steakhouse not to far from the marina. We freshened up and changed into dinner clothes. I applied some makeup and decided to leave my hair down, long and curly. I wore a white, Capri jumper with an open back. I accessorized it with black high heels, and a small black handbag. Carter wore grey suit with a white button down shirt.

Everyone looked stunning. Ray and Stone drove us to the steakhouse in two separate cars. The girls wanted to travel together in Ray's car. The boys traveled in Stone's car. Carter did not like the idea of driving in separate cars but Becky and Sam thought it would be a great idea. Carter gave me a long kiss before helping me into Ray's vehicle. "See you in a few minutes, Ma Cerise." Becky and Sam giggled like teenagers beside me. His sexy walk made my clit throb. His dirty blond hair was so soft and brushed back with his fingers. He was perfectly dressed and you could see his muscular body underneath his clothes. My body wanted his.

"You guys make such a great couple," Sam complimented.

"Thank you. I think so too." I stared out the window, at Carter, as he walked to Stone's car.

"Seventeen years in the making! Was it worth the wait?" Becky asked.

"Yes, definitely, he is an incredible man. It feels like we have always been together," I explained.

"In our eyes, you guys have always been together too. Except in a more secretive, discrete way," Sam stated.

"You guys can't keep your hands off one another. Carter has always looked at you fondly and was always there when you needed him, but he has changed. He is infatuated with you. You see his love written all over his face," Becky added.

"He makes me happy." I paused. "I'm sure it's the same for both of you. Sam, you and Kyle have an amazing relationship. How do you do it after all these years?"

"We make sure we take time for us, to be a couple, not just parents. Between his shift work and raising kids, it is not easy. It's important to make time for each other." She looked down at her wedding ring. "It doesn't hurt that our SEX life is AMAZING too." We laughed. We did not expect that from our quiet Samantha.

"Becky, you and Mike are hot for each other too. I do not think, I have seen you this happy with anyone before. What's the scoop?" I asked.

"Mike is different. First, he is two years older than I am. He is well established. He is serious about me. Look at him, he is good looking and has a killer body. We love to run together. Oh yeah, and the SEX is AMAZING." We started to laugh even harder. I began to wonder what Ray was thinking while he listened to our conversation.

"Cerise, cough it up. How's your sex life?" Becky asked boldly.

"Its fun, exciting, breathtaking, and nothing short of AMAZING." I was not going to elaborate with details with Ray sitting in the front seat. I have to live with him everyday too. Becky was sitting in the middle. She took Sam's hand and my hand in her own and gave them a tight squeeze. "I'm so happy for you guys. I think we are finally feeling true happiness. That's all I've ever wanted, for all of us." We leaned over and hugged each other.

"We are almost there. No crying, we will ruin our makeup. I love you guys," Sam cried.

"I love you guys too," I added. They had been my best friends since elementary school.

"We're here, ladies. I could drive around the block if you need another minute," Ray interrupted.

"No, we are good. We were having a girl moment," I confessed.

"I understand. My daughter has those moments often with her friends, too."

We pulled up to the front of the restaurant. Carter was there to open up my door, to help me out. "How was your drive? Talk about anything interesting?" he asked.

"Well, the drive was AMAZING." I giggled and looked at Sam and Becky. "The topic of conversation was interesting." I gave him a kiss quickly then walked to the sidewalk where Kyle, Mike, and Stone were standing. Carter helped Becky and Sam out of the car as well. Carter came to my side and held my hand.

We waited there briefly while Ray parked his car. When he joined us, we entered the restaurant. Carter had called earlier to make a reservation. The restaurant host smiled at Carter and lead the way to a private party room in the back. It was obvious she was attracted to Carter. He seemed unaware of the constant stares from girls. We walked hand in hand to a private room, with French doors. It was in the back corner of the restaurant. The lighting was dim and the table was set beautifully with candles. I was here once before. Carter took me to *The Phantom of the Opera* for my birthday many years ago. We came to this restaurant for dinner, before going to the theatre. The restaurant also had private booths, for two or four people, with a curtain for privacy. I did not know they had a private party room. It was beautiful.

Dinner was delicious. We had a wonderful evening with our friends. Carter invited Ray and Stone to eat with us, as well. Carter stood up. He bent down and gently kissed me. He looked a little nervous. I looked at him and whispered, "Are you okay?" He nodded yes. He had everyone's attention without even asking for it.

"Thank you for coming to dinner and spending time with us this weekend. It means so much to Cerise and I. Cerise and I have known each other for seventeen years. I always had a crush on Cerise in high school, but it was ten years ago in this restaurant, I knew I wanted to spend the rest of my life with her." He looked down at me, with a nervous smile. I wondered where he was going with this.

"We were sitting in one of the private booths, outside this room. I was taking her to see *The Phantom of the Opera* for her birthday. I remember our conversation, as if it were yesterday. She said to me, 'Carter, the girl you choose to marry will be the luckiest girl, in the world.' I hope you still feel that way," Carter smiled nervously. He kneeled down on one knee. I was holding back the tears. I knew exactly where he was going with his speech. "I would be the luckiest man in the world, if you'd marry me. Will you marry me, Ma Cerise?"

He pulled out a ring box to show me the ring. Before I could even look at it, I jumped into his arms. "Yes, I will marry you!" I began to cry and laugh, at the same time. I kissed him gently. He smiled and took my hand and put the ring on my finger. It was the most beautiful ring I have ever seen. It was white gold and had a radiant cut solitaire diamond. It was flawless. It sparkled so much. I could not stop looking at it. I gave Carter another kiss. "It is beautiful. I love it."

Everyone started to clap and gathered around, to congratulate us. Sam and Becky loved my ring. They both gave me a tight hug. Sam pulled out her camera and started to take pictures of us. We posed for a few of them, but the rest were spontaneous shots. I was thankful she had her camera with her, to capture Carter's proposal. Everyone sat down again when the server came in with coffee, tea, and dessert. I sat closer to Carter and put my left hand on his. My engagement ring sparkled at us. I whispered to him, "I am the luckiest woman in the world."

He smiled and kissed me softly.

Chapter Nineteen

The morning was quiet. I listened to the gentle waves as they rolled towards shore and splashed against the side of the yacht. Recently, it has become one of my favorite sounds. I loved the view of the lake. We had a beautiful location, to dock our boat. It was the last spot on the dock, so nothing obstructed the view of the water. I sat up in the corner with my feet up and drank my tea. My ring caught my eye often. It seemed surreal. Everything had been happening so fast. I was wearing my new pajama set, which Carter bought me. It was a pale pink set: Capri pants, camisole, and a cotton three-quarter sleeve cover-up. It fit perfectly. It was casual, but sexy at the same time without being lacy and sheer. I pulled my hair into a high ponytail.

Carter greeted me as he came up on deck to join me, with his coffee in hand. "Somehow I knew, you would find a special place of your own on our boat," he smiled.

"Yes, I think this is it. It has a perfect view of the lake," I scanned my view. "It is even better with you sitting there." I winked at him. He wore only pajama bottoms, which hung low off his hips. If my eyes could undress him, he would have been sitting naked. He moved closer to me. I held my breath, when he touched my knee and slid his hand up my thigh.

"I can't wait for you to be Mrs. Blake," he whispered softly.

"Me too." I smiled and looked at my ring. "This ring is beautiful. You have exquisite taste."

"When I saw it for the first time, I knew you would love it. One of my clients has a chain of jewelry stores across Canada. I asked him to drop by my office with a few of his one-of-a-kind pieces of jewelry. I fell in love, with this one," he explained.

"Thank you, Carter. I love it. I'm almost afraid to wear it." I admired my ring.

"I do not want you to take it off. It is a token of my never ending love." He kissed my hand then my ring. "I love you, always have."

"Carter, I love you too. I have never been happier in my whole life." I positioned myself on his lap. "I hope I can make you as happy, as you make me."

"You do. Now we need to make wedding plans, which is the fun part," he smiled. "If you need it, my mom would love to help. She helped plan my brother's wedding, and it was perfect."

"Do you want a big wedding?" I asked.

"Usually it's expected in my family, but it does not have to be. I have no preference. What would you like, a big or small wedding?" he asked.

"I have to think about it. I do not have any family, just my close friends. I don't even have parents to give me away in a traditional wedding."

"It does not have to be traditional."

"You make everything seem so simple. That's what I love about you," I said sincerely.

"We'll do it our way. First step is a date. Any ideas?"

"If it's a traditional wedding, then we would probably need a year to plan. If it's a nontraditional wedding it could be sooner," I answered.

"Okay I'm liking the nontraditional wedding already," Carter laughed. "The sooner the better." He kissed my neck playfully.

"A friend of mine traveled to the Caribbean to get married, with close family and friends in attendance. When they returned they had a reception with extended family and friends. Would you consider looking into a destination wedding?"

"Great idea, let's look into it. Anything for you." He kissed me harder this time, with more lust.

"Get a room!" Kyle joked as he came up on deck, followed by Sam. Kyle patted Carter's shoulder and sat down beside him.

"It's so beautiful and calm in the morning." Sam stood there looking at the water, in awe of the view. She sipped her coffee slowly.

"I would love to download your pictures off your camera, onto my computer. Would you mind if I did?" I asked.

"Sure! I was going to ask you to do it." She retrieved her camera and USB wire, to download the pictures. We balanced my computer on both of our legs as the pictures began to download. There were about a hundred and fifty pictures of our day together. Once downloaded, we started to look at each one. We laughed at the pictures taken on Mike's bike. They turned out good; some were better than others. Once we looked through the pictures, Carter and Kyle took my computer to look at the pictures themselves.

"This one I need as my screensaver at work," Carter laughed. I looked over to see what picture got his attention. It was the picture of me lying across the bike with one leg bent and my back arched. It was a picture of me wearing the black bikini, which Carter bought me. I smacked his arm playfully. "I'm serious," he smiled. "This is an amazing picture. I do not know how much work I would get done, but I would be the envy of the office," he laughed. I blew him a kiss.

Sam and I started to talk about her girls, Hannah and Savannah. They stayed with Sam's parents for the night. They loved going there. Grandma and Grandpa spoil them rotten.

"Ma Cerise, this has to be our engagement picture." He encouraged me to come back to look at the screen. I leaned over to look at the picture. It was of the two of us on the bike face-to-face, with my back arched back and his lips between my breasts.

"Yeah, I'm sure that will go over well. It will be such a proud moment for your parents." I kissed his forehead. "Actually, go to picture 132. I love this picture of us. It would be a great engagement picture." It was a picture of us, after Carter proposed. We did not pose for this picture. It was a natural picture of us smiling and looking into each other's eyes.

"I agree. It's a beautiful picture," Sam said. "You can even print it in black and white or sepia to change the effect."

"I love it too. Great choice," Carter agreed. "Sam, you're a great photographer. Have you ever considered starting a business in photography?"

"I have considered it. Once the girls are in school full-time, I think I will go back to work," Sam said.

"That will be so exciting." I wanted the best for her. "I can help you start up your business."

Becky and Mike joined us. It looked like they had had sex. Their hair was messy and they were holding hands and shared a secretive look. Becky gave us hugs. She sat down and Carter passed her my computer. "Cerise and Sam downloaded the pictures from yesterday. I'm sure you will love them."

Carter was right. Becky loved them. She made comments on the same pictures, Carter liked. She tried to persuade everyone to sell the pictures to Harley Davidson's advertising department. She felt the pictures were a great photo-shoot. This was her line of business, so she knew what she was talking about with her experience. Sam and I were the hesitant ones. We were not used to the limelight. She also agreed, the picture we picked for our engagement picture shouted happiness and love.

Once we ate breakfast, we changed and walked along the boardwalk. It was such a beautiful morning. The sun was hot, there was a soft breeze off the water, and birds were singing. We had a wonderful morning with our friends.

Everyone left around 11:00 a.m. Carter and I tidied up and made the beds. Carter was in a playful mood. He tried to lift my skirt to see if I was wearing panties, or if it was a skort. I was playing hard to get and did not let him see. He chased me around but I managed to always escape his hold.

We heard his mom and dad on deck, calling Carter's name, so I ran over to the stairs. I climbed up knowing, Carter was looking up my skirt. I flicked my skirt up to show him what I was wearing underneath...His facial expression was priceless when he seen my lacy white thong.

"Oh man, there's always interruptions," he muttered under his breath. I giggled and continued to climb the ladder.

"Hello, Mr. and Mrs. Blake," I greeted.

"I hope we are not interrupting anything, we heard laughter," Mrs. Blake apologized.

"No, we were cleaning up downstairs. We had our friends stay over last night," Carter lied about the interruption. He shook his dad's hand and kissed his mom's cheek. "I'm so glad you stopped by. We have some news we'd like to share with you."

"We hope its good news." Mrs. Blake knew how stressful the past week has been on both of us. Good news would be a blessing.

"Cerise and I are engaged. I proposed to her last night," he announced. He was holding my hand and gave it a tight squeeze.

"Congratulations!" They said together. Mrs. Blake was emotional. She hugged me and kissed her son on the cheek. Mr. Blake shook Carter's hand, pulled him in for a bear hug.

"Wonderful news!" Mrs. Blake showed emotion in her eyes, but held her tears back. "I'm so excited for both of you. Have you set a date?"

"No, not yet! Soon." Carter disclosed.

"This is something we need to celebrate. We would love to take you out to lunch. We were going to go to the yacht club. Please join us," Mrs. Blake asked.

"Am I underdressed?" I asked. I was wearing a navy, casual mini skirt and white tank top with blue flowered embroidery around the neck.

"No, you are fine, dear. They request no jeans or swimwear during the day. Evenings are different, as it's a little more dressy," she answered.

"I think you're dressed perfectly to go to the yacht club," Carter added with his devilish smile. He was referring to my panties. "We would love to join you."

I grabbed my white sandals. Carter quickly changed below deck. When he returned he was wearing cotton navy pants and a white golf shirt. Both, he bought at Tommy Hilfiger. Max and Jagger were on the dock when we left. Carter informed them where we were going and the approximate time of return. He felt it was not necessary to have them tag along since we were not going far and we were going to lunch at a member's only yacht club. I guess he figured my stalker would not be a member, therefore would not be allowed in.

We had a lovely lunch with Carter's parents. Mrs. Blake admired my ring and offered to help with the wedding plans. I accepted, as I did not know the first thing about planning a wedding. She was beyond thrilled about the news of her first grandchild in February, and now there was a wedding to plan. She was a wonderful woman. She was elegant and well respected. She was well educated, however, she choose not to work professionally. She stayed home to raise her three children. Once they became more independent, she became the head of many social committees. She held many fundraisers and organized social events. Her wealth did not affect her kind heart.

Mrs. Blake gave me some homework to do. She referred me to a few websites to check out for wedding receptions. She wanted me to first decide on an approximate date. Then narrow down the venues. She assured me, the rest would fall into place thereafter.

❀

We stayed an extra night on the yacht. Monday was the Labor Day statutory holiday. Usually, I spent long weekends working but being with Carter made me forget about work and enjoy my long weekend with him. We spent most of the afternoon and early evening researching the websites Mrs. Blake suggested. We researched the top twenty wedding venues, in the Toronto area, on the Internet. We narrowed down our list, to a few elegant locations in Toronto. Most were beautiful and elegant, but lacked individuality. I fell in love with Casa Loma immediately. I loved castles, so this fit my personality perfectly. Casa Loma was mysterious, beautiful, and had so much character. Carter and I wanted to visit the locations on our short list of venues, in person, before we made our final decision. We explored the possibility of going south to get married and having a reception when we return, as well. There were so many beautiful resorts, for destination weddings.

"Casa Loma is a tourist attraction. Do you want to go tomorrow and walk around the grounds? If we're lucky maybe a wedding coordinator will be there to answer a few questions."

"I would love to. I love castles. I think they're so romantic." I had a giddy sound to my voice.

"I love seeing you this excited about planning our wedding. You will be a beautiful bride," he complimented.

"And you will be a handsome groom."

Carter leaned over to give me a kiss. He started to caress my arm and pull me in closer to him. "Are you cold? The temperature has dropped. Let me get you a blanket." He retrieved a fleece blanket from the cabin. When he returned he had the blanket and two glasses of red wine. He put the wine glasses down, sat down beside me, and covered both of us up in the blanket, before handing me the wine glass.

"In two and half months we will be on a cruise in the Caribbean. The sunsets will be incredible to watch with you."

"I can only imagine how beautiful it will be. I cannot wait. We leave Monday, November 17, right? I better put the date in my schedule, so I don't make any appointments."

"Yeah, I'm looking forward to having you to myself without any interruptions." He started to run his hands up my legs under the blanket. "I have some unfinished business from this morning." He wore his devilish smile.

"I thought you forgot. It has been twenty-four hours since you proposed to me and you haven't been able to get in my panties," I laughed. "Maybe we should wait until we are married!"

136

"Then we better get married tonight. I won't be able to wait a year." His hands were inching their way up my inner thigh. He reached my panties and started to take them off. "I really liked looking up your skirt earlier today."

"I thought you would."

He took my panties off and put them on his head. "How do they look on me?" he joked playfully.

"Stop. Someone is going to see you," I laughed. He did not take them off. He could be such a jokester. He pulled the covers over his head and started to kiss his way up my thigh. I opened my legs wider for him to get closer. I leaned back into my corner and enjoyed my arousal. His tongue, fingers, and lips were busy pleasuring me. I began to moan softly. I heard footsteps. I tensed "Carter!" I whispered. I started to close my legs, but Carter pushed them open. "Carter!" I tapped him on the back of his head. "Carter!" The blanket covered Carter's body. He probably did not hear me or thought I was saying his name in pleasure.

Stone climbed the stairs to the upper deck. "Is Mr. Blake around? I need to talk to him."

Startled, by Stone's voice, Carter jumped out from underneath the blanket. Stone's face said everything. His eyes were wide and his mouth opened automatically, in embarrassment.

"Oh, I'm sorry to interrupt." Stone quickly climbed down the stairs. We heard him laughing and talking to Ray in the distance. I gave Carter a look of embarrassment and sighed.

"What? It was not obvious what I was doing. Was it?" he joked. "I could have been looking for your earrings," he suggested.

"Maybe he thought you are Houdini," I laughed.

"Why?"

"Because you managed to take my panties off and put them on your head, while looking for my earrings," I laughed uncontrollably. I laughed so hard tears were rolling down my cheeks and I could not breath. "Your hair is so messy and sticking through the lace holes. Priceless!" I reached for my phone. "I have to get a picture," I giggled.

He grabbed my wrists and held them together with one hand, to prevent me from grabbing my phone. His other hand tickled me until I surrendered. Still holding my hands together, he unzipped his pants and slid his cock into me. *I should tease him more often…. I enjoyed my punishment,* I thought.

Chapter Twenty

I was in awe of the castle. Casa Loma was big, exquisite and had so much history. I loved learning about its history during our tour. We walked through the castle's different rooms. Each room was unique in their own way. I loved the library room. The dark wood bookshelves lined the entire wall— breathtaking. Glass-paneled doors covered the bookshelves. Through those doors, you could see old books. The conservatory was beautiful. It was bright and had plants along each side. It would be perfect for our wedding ceremony. The well-maintained garden was fabulous. *I had a vision of women from the early 1900s era, in their dresses, feather hats, and umbrellas walking through the garden, with their hand in a gentleman's arm, for a stroll. The men wore dark suits, a hat, and using a cane for fashion purpose only.* The 800-foot tunnels lead us to the stables. The tunnel was dark, humid, and had an unexplained eerie atmosphere.

We returned to the conservatory, after our tour. I took in every detail. It reminded me of a Mediterranean courtyard with beautiful, shiny marble floors. I loved the gothic-style windows. I could not stop looking up at the Italian stained glass domed ceiling. "This is so beautiful. What do you think?" I asked.

"It is perfect. It is different from any other wedding venue I have been to before."

"Online I read Casa Loma can accommodate up to 200 hundred people for a sit down dinner, or 550 people for a stand up reception. I like the idea of a smaller wedding. I also love we could have the ceremony, pictures, and the reception under one roof. What do you think about having the ceremony here? Or, would you prefer a church wedding?" I asked.

"It does not have to be a church wedding. They can recommend a minister to come here. The conservatory can be set up with chairs, covered with chair linens and flowers to make it elegant. Mom would know who to call." He sounded experienced in making formal arrangements. I guess in a way, he was, as he has been organizing the gala each year for the last five years.

"The reception can be in the library. The surroundings are so unique. Not your typical banquet room." I continued to look at the unique details around the room.

"Sounds like you love this place."

"I do. There is something about this place, which is drawing me in. Maybe it makes me feel like a princess." I giggled and spun around, looking at the ceiling. Carter grabbed me and held me close. There were other people walking through the castle, but Carter did not seem to mind. Carter picked me up, held me around my waist, and spun me around a few times. He put me down and kissed me.

"I don't think we need to see any other venues. This one seems perfect for us. I know you love it, and that's what matters to me," Carter smiled.

"Are you sure? I'm sure the other places are beautiful too," I asked.

"I'm sure. I want you to be happy," he smiled softly.

"I am happy. I love this place." I kissed him and hugged him around his neck. "Do you think your Mom will approve?"

"Of course. This is one of her favorite places too," he replied.

"Excuse me. Are you the couple interested in getting information about having a wedding here?" A woman in a grey two-piece suit asked.

"Yes, I am Carter Blake and this is Cerise Brooks. We left our name at the front desk," Carter answered.

"My name is Patricia Reid. I'm the wedding and event planner here. Would you like to come to my office? I have some time to talk to you if you'd like," she offered.

"Thank you, we'd love to."

We followed her to her office. It was at the front entrance of the building. She answered our questions and gave us a package to take home. She was professional and friendly. She must have been doing this for a number of years, as she knew so much about the history of the castle and everything there was to know about planning a wedding of our dreams. I was not one of those little girls, who dreamt of a large wedding. Those dreams did not seem realistic to me, as a child. However, as I sat there talking with Patricia, I felt like a little girl dressing up and marrying her Prince Charming.

"We are interested in having our wedding here at Casa Loma. What are your available dates?" Carter asked.

"Typically we book twelve to eighteen months in advance, especially on Saturdays. They book fast for weddings. Let me grab my event schedule. Excuse me." She turned around, walked over to another table in her office, and returned with a scheduling book in her hand. "Actually, I came in today because I had a couple cancel their wedding. It was scheduled two and half months from now, so I came in today to notify and cancel services which were booked for them." She paused and started to look through her book. "What month would you like to get married in?"

"We're open. What's your availability for late August or early September next year?" I asked.

"We have a couple dates available. We have the last Saturday in August and the second Saturday in September." Carter and I looked at each other, trying to read each other's minds.

"Out of curiosity, what date was your cancellation on?" Carter asked.

"It was Saturday, November 15th," she answered.

Carter looked over at me, and smiled. "Do you think we could have a private moment to discuss this?" he asked Patricia.

"Sure, I will check on the staff at the front." She left her office and closed the door.

"What do you think about having our wedding on November 15th? We're leaving for our cruise on the seventeenth, so it would be perfect timing to leave on vacation two days later." Carter suggested. "I know it's your birthday gift. We can plan a separate vacation in the new year to go to Italy, Greece, or Bora Bora or some place of your choice."

"Do you think planning a wedding in this timeframe is possible?" I asked. My heart started to race.

"Yes, I don't see a problem with it," he answered with confidence.

"Okay, let's book it!" Excitement grew within me. I felt like I was going to explode with happiness. "People are going to think I'm pregnant," I laughed.

"I'm hoping we will be soon," he kissed me.

"Have you decided what date will work with your plans?" Patricia asked when she entered her office.

"Yes, We would like to book the 15th of November," Carter answered.

"Really? In all the years I have been working here, this has never happened before. It is meant to be."

"That's the way I see it too," Carter smiled. "It is meant to be." He looked at me and squeezed my hand gently.

"The next couple of months will be busy for you. In the first couple of weeks, you will have to arrange the flowers, caterer, linens, table decorations, invitations, etc. Then your focus will be on your dress for you and your bridesmaids. If you need help, let me know," Patricia offered.

"Thank you. I do have someone to help with the arrangements. She will probably be in touch with you soon. She is my future mother-in-law," I told her.

"Wonderful. What is her name? I will put her name down as a contact to release and discuss your wedding plans," she asked.

We gave her the information she required and paid the deposit. A couple of hours had passed since we first arrived. We left, hand in hand. The reality of getting married was starting to sink in. Jagger and Max were waiting outside, by the car. They could see our smiles a mile away.

"By the look on your faces. This is the place. When's the big day?" Jagger asked.

"November 15th," Carter answered.

"Fifteen month engagement...how will you survive?" Jagger joked.

We both laughed. "I couldn't survive, so we chose this year," Carter announced.

We drove back to the marina. On the way, we made a stop at a gas station to grab wedding magazines to look for ideas. I was excited to share our news with Carter's parents, so Carter instructed Jagger and Max to head back to our yacht. We planned to meet them back there in thirty minutes. We walked two docks over to Carter's parents yacht. It was my first time visiting them on their yacht. It was beautiful. It was about ten feet longer than ours was. It had a slightly different layout and was bigger below deck, compared to ours.

"We have decided on where our wedding will take place," Carter announced.

"That was fast. Where is this beautiful wedding going to take place?" Mrs. Blake asked.

"Casa Loma," I said proudly.

"It's a beautiful castle. I assume they were booked well over a year in advance," she assumed.

"Usually yes... They had a cancellation and we booked it on that date," Carter explained.

"Oh? When?" Mrs. Blake asked.

"November 15th, this year," I advised. "Will you help me with the arrangements? It's a short time to do everything."

"This is wonderful news. We have to start this week. First will be the invitations. We have to get them sent to the printer right away."

She was excited for us. She made a to-do-list and arranged it in priority order. I felt comfortable knowing I had Mrs. Blake helping me plan our special day. You could tell she thoroughly loved planning events, especially for her son's wedding. We looked through the magazines I bought, and she jotted down my ideas and visions of how I wanted the ceremony and reception to be. She wanted each decision to be ours. It was thrilling to see our ideas on paper.

Carter received a phone call. I figured it was Jagger or Max following up on our whereabouts. We had been gone longer than we expected. He looked distracted. He walked to the other side of the yacht to get some privacy. When he returned, he had a brief conversation with Mr. Blake. Both of them had a worried look.

"Carter, Is everything okay?"

"I don't want you to worry about it," he answered.

"Carter, what is it?" I stood up to stand beside him.

"Ray was at the apartment, to check everything before we returned today." He looked down at me tenderly. "No one broke in. However, another envelope was left taped to the door," he explained. Jagger and Max arrived at Mr. and Mrs. Blake's Yacht.

"What did the note say?" I was afraid to ask.

"SOON!" Carter answered in a low voice. I began to cry. He hugged me and rubbed my back. "It's okay. We are going to catch whoever it is. Ray and Kyle are watching the surveillance videos right now."

"Darling, you are going to be fine. Let's focus on the positive and let everyone else do the worrying," Mrs. Blake stood behind me and started to rub my back. Carter had kept them informed on everything that had happened. They had been supportive.

My hands were shaking uncontrollably. My heart was beating so fast, I could hear the beating in my ears. I wished it would go away magically. How could my life be so complete one minute and upside down the next? I was finally happy and yet I had this dangerous black cloud hanging over each step I took. I had not been back to my own apartment in over a week. In fact, I have not been alone anywhere, in over a week. This was so crazy. I lived on my own for years, coming and going as I pleased. I felt restricted, confined, and caged.

I felt weak in my knees. My eyes darkened. I held onto Carter and whispered through my tears, "I'm not feeling well." I spoke weakly and fainted.

Chapter Twenty-One

My mind was on everything else but work. I had spent the morning trying to concentrate on the merger. I prepared my notes, to discuss with Mr. Walker, at our meeting scheduled for the following day. I was a mess, due to a sleepless night and my increased jumpiness. I would rather be in a dark hole, than pretend everything was normal. Kyle and Scott advised it was important to continue my normal routine. It was actually harder, than I thought.

After I fainted, Carter catered to my needs, more than he had before. He argued with Kyle about me going to work. He felt it was getting increasingly dangerous for me. Carter has been helpful and protective during the ordeal.

Carter had texted me several times, to see how I was feeling. Even during this stressful time, Carter managed to make me smile with his tenderness and thoughtfulness.

I had no appetite but picked at a salad, Max had bought me. Carter asked him to buy me lunch. Normally Carter would come for lunch but he had a lunch meeting. My phone startled me, when it rang. I grabbed my phone and answered it quickly. It was Alec. *Why did I have to answer the phone?* I avoided him and dealt with Mr. Walker, only.

"You're alive." Alec said. He did not realize how bad of a joke it was, and I was not about to explain it to him either.

"Hello, Alec. What can I do for you?" I said coldly.

"No warm greeting or I missed you."

"I'm busy. Did you call to harass me? Or is there a reason why you called?"

"Ok, enough with the small talk then. The meeting has been changed to this afternoon at three o'clock."

"My meeting with Mr. Walker?"

"Yes, technically it's with both of us."

"I'm not falling for that one again. Why didn't Mr. Walker call?"

"He's busy, so I told him I would call." Without seeing him, I knew he was wearing his cocky grin. "Meet us at the French Bistro, close to your office building, at three o'clock. Don't be late." Then he hung up the phone. I stared at my phone for a few minutes. I could not believe he hung up on me. *Should I trust him?* I thought. After his last meeting stunt, I could not take a chance. I promised Carter I would not be alone with him. I dialed Mr. Walker's phone number to confirm the meeting plans. Mr. Walker confirmed the meeting with me and apologized for changing it last minute. It turned out he had to fly out of town in the morning, for a last minute business trip. I felt much better after I talked to him. I started to prepare my files and notes to take to the meeting. With only two hours before my meeting, I found myself rushing around to make up for lost time.

I arrived at the restaurant fifteen minutes early. Max and Jagger walked me to the restaurant. They sat at an outdoor patio table after checking the restaurant. Inside, both Mr. Walker and Alec greeted me. Alec was professional and business like. It bugged me. Most people would not believe me, if I told them how he spoke to me. He used his power and authority to his advantage. We had discussed our business matter, over a late lunch. Both Mr. Walker and Alec seemed to be happy with my progress. Since moving into my office, I reviewed the files and prepared my analysis at a faster pace, than originally expected. It looked as though, I might finish ahead of time.

Mr. Walker excused himself to go to the restroom. As soon as he was far enough away from the table, Alec said, "You look a little tired. Need a neck massage?"

"Alec, why do you do that? You can be so nice one minute then turn into a total creep the next."

"I'm not being creepy. I'm concerned."

"You have a strange way of showing it."

"If you let me, I can show you how concerned I am. I can be caring, generous, and I'm great in bed."

"No, thanks!" I stood up. "Please tell Mr. Walker you were a jerk, so I had to leave." I walked out of the restaurant. Jagger and Max were at the same table and stood up soon when they seen me.

"Cerise!" Alec called out. He was one step behind me.

"Our meeting is over," I grumbled rudely.

"I'm sorry." Then he grabbed me and kissed me in public. He would not let me go. My arms were held tightly underneath his. I heard tires screech on the road behind me. I could not see anything but it crossed my mind that it was my stalker. The screeching sound was so loud; I thought the car was going to hit us on the sidewalk. Max and Jagger pulled Alec off me. Jagger was getting up close to Alec's face and asked him what he was doing. He shoved Alec a couple of times. If I had a brother, I pictured he would do the same to protect me from a bully. Max made sure I was okay.

"Cerise I can't believe you would deceive our business contract in this way." Mr. Walker looked disappointed as he walked towards me. "If I knew you had romantic feelings for Alec, I would not have hired you in the first place. I wanted an unbiased opinion, not an influenced opinion. I have a lot of money at stake here."

"Mr. Walker, I can assure you there are no romantic feeling on my part. And the opinion I give will be my professional unbiased opinion," I pleaded.

"I'm sorry, Cerise. I'm withdrawing from our contract."

"Mr. Walker, please don't do this. I've worked hard, and I haven't done anything wrong."

"It appears the two of you have been colluding, to make this merger beneficial in Alec's favor."

"Mr. Walker, I'd like the opportunity to explain everything."

"No need, my mind is made up. I will ensure you are compensated in full, based on our contract." Mr. Walker turned and walked down the sidewalk towards the public parking lot.

I could not believe what happened. I was fired. *Could my life get any worse?* I thought.

"Cerise, I'm sorry," Alec pleaded.

"Are you? You disgust me!" I slapped Alec across the face so hard my hand stung.

I had to get out of there. I ran up the street towards my office building. Jagger and Max ran after me. I could not control my emotions anymore. I sat on a bench located outside my office building and sobbed with my face in my hands. My dream opportunity was gone. It slipped through my fingers. My reputation would be ruined, if this leaked out to the media.

Jagger and Max sat beside me. They did not say a word. They did not sympathize or try to console me. I did not want to talk to anyone. My face was still resting in my hands when I heard footsteps approach and stop right in front of me. I slowly looked up. It was Carter. I stood up and reached out to hug him. I was happy to see him, but he was not happy to see me. His facial expression was angry and disappointed.

"You had me fooled," Carter growled.

"What?"

"Goes to show you, you really do not know someone. I really thought you were different from the Jenna's in the world."

"Carter, what's going on?"

"I saw you kissing Alec." He put his fingers through his hair out of frustration. "I was driving by and saw you. I trusted you. You knew how I felt about Alec." It started to make sense. The screeching tires I heard must have been Carter.

"It is a misunderstanding. Let me explain."

"Don't bother. Nothing you say can make me trust you again." He put his fingers through his hair again. "Please have your belongings moved out by tomorrow."

"Carter!" I reached out and touched his chest. He took my hand off chest and dropped it.

"Please don't. This is hard enough." His eyes looked glossy. "I'll stay somewhere else tonight." He turned and walked away.

"Carter!" I yelled. "Let me explain."

Chapter Twenty-Two

Was I in the Twilight Zone? I was happily in love and planning my wedding. Then with a blink of an eye, it was over. I had lost the love of my life and my career opportunity. I moved back into my lonely apartment. I had not been alone since Carter and I first made love. I was scared, lonely, confused, and depressed. It had been two days since I last spoke to Carter. He would not take my calls or reply to my texts. I wrote him a long text explaining everything. I expressed how sorry I was for hurting him. I knew he read my text messages. He did not believe me.

I did not return to my office. I had no work to do. I had no desire to go. I had been in my pajamas for two days watching TV. A mouth-watering hamburger commercial aired on the TV, which made my stomach growl. I did not eat anything either. Black tea or water was the only thing I had in my apartment. I had been away from my apartment for two weeks and did not have any food in my fridge or cupboards. I had no desire to go grocery shopping. I knew I had to eventually but at that moment, I did not care.

Carter must have relieved Ray and his security staff of their duties, as well. I did not see or hear from anyone. Even if I wanted to go to the grocery store, I had fear of leaving my apartment. I could not get the nerve to go out. I should have called Rebecca or Samantha. I was sure they would have gone to the store with me. They left messages but I had not returned their phone calls. I knew they were worried about me. What would I say to them? *I screwed up! My life is over! No Fiancée! No Career! No happiness! I lost everything good in my life!*

I spent an entire week in my apartment. I did not leave once. I ordered fast food a few times during the week. I was sick of having pizza for breakfast, lunch, and dinner. I did not want to see another pizza ever again.

I slipped out of the shower, put my robe on, and wrapped a towel around my hair. It felt good to take a long, hot shower. There was a knock at the door. My heart raced. Who could it be? I tiptoed to the door to look through the peephole. It was Sam and Becky. I opened the door and gave them a hug. Instantly the tears began to flow.

"Why haven't you returned our calls?" Sam asked.

"I've been busy."

"Busy watching TV and feeling sorry for yourself." Becky mumbled.

"If you're here to tell me how terrible I am, I've heard it already."

"We're here because we're worried about you," Sam admitted.

Becky started to sort through the takeout containers and clean up the garbage I left around all week. She shook her head, from time to time, in disbelief.

"You look like shit!" Becky commented.

"Becky! Don't be so hard on her," Sam argued.

"I don't know what Carter told you but he has it wrong. I did not cheat on him. Alec kissed me and I pushed him off and slapped him in the face. Carter didn't see that part." I began to cry. "Its over! He will not believe me. It does not matter what the truth is anyway. Mr. Walker thinks I was colluding, with Alec. Carter thinks I cheated on him, with Alec. I lost my contract, and, to make it worse, when I go back to my office tomorrow, there is a chance I will bump into Carter at one point or another. How awkward will that be?"

"You can't think about it. You have to focus on getting yourself back to normal," Sam encouraged.

"What is normal?"

"Well, first thing first. We are going to get you some groceries. Then we're going to the mall to get your hair and nails done," Becky demanded. "I believe you, Cerise. If Carter doesn't, then it's his loss."

"I know you wouldn't cheat on Carter. Alec made it seem that way. I knew he was trouble from the first time we saw him," Sam stated. "If it makes you feel any better, Carter has been a wreck all week, too. Kyle took him out for a drink on Friday night to change his mind."

"Did Kyle say anything else?" I asked.

"He's hurt because..." Sam started to explain. I stared at her for a moment, prompting her to continue. "He thought you were the one person in this world who he could trust."

The words hurt more than an actual stab wound to the heart. I began to sob. *How could I let this happen? I really thought I could handle everything. I was wrong. Alec's personality and his vindictive desire to hurt Carter were too much for me to handle. I was too stubborn to notice I was sacrificing the only thing that made me truly happy... Carter!*

"Sam! Look what you have done. Why did you have to tell her?" Becky scolded. "We are a poor excuse for friends. We came here to cheer you up but instead I've criticized the way you look and Sam is telling you details about Carter." She sat down beside me and gave me a hug. Sam joined in.

"I really appreciate you both coming here. I am not great company today. I have lost my boyfriend and best friend. It hurts so badly. This was why I didn't want to date him in the first place." I blew my nose. "I knew if it didn't work out, I would lose him completely, out of my life, forever."

"He'll come around," Sam tried to be positive to spare my feelings.

"I don't think so. You did not see the way he looked at me. He hates me." I took a deep breath to control the tears from flowing. "He won't even return my texts or calls."

"Then he's the one being immature, and it's his loss," Becky said coldly. "Let's get you out of this place. You'll feel much better with some fresh air."

She was right. I felt better after getting some fresh air, a balanced meal, and some retail therapy. They actually had me laughing, by the end of the day. The sadness was still there weighing heavily on my heart, but I felt it was the first step to pulling me together.

My office was lonely. No security staff watched over me. No lunch dates with Carter. No quickies on the boardroom table.

I waited for the elevator on Thursday night. The elevator bell rang, indicating the elevator arrived. I fumbled around with my briefcase and keys and walked into the elevator. I requested, "Ground, please!" I looked up to say thank you, then realized it was Carter. It had been a couple of weeks since we had spoke or seen each other. My heart sank into my stomach. He was so handsome standing there in his navy blue suit, white shirt, and tie. His hair looked like he ran his fingers through it, as he always did.

"Carter! Nice to see you," I did not know what else to say.

He nodded with pressed lips. "Wish I could say the same."

"Carter, can we go somewhere and talk?"

"Not a good idea! It is best if we move on. Nothing will change the way I feel about you and what you did."

"Please give me a chance to explain." The elevator bell chimed and the doors opened to the lobby. Carter exited the elevator. I followed him out. I was wounded by his words. It took everything in me to control my emotions.

He approached a beautiful woman in the lobby and greeted her with a kiss on her cheek. She was happy to see Carter and linked her arm in his, when they left the building. They piled into his car, parked out front. I could see Phillip in the driver seat waiting for them. Carter opened the door for his date to get in the car. As he walked to the other side, we made eye contact. At that moment, I knew there was no hope to reconcile. It was over.

Chapter Twenty-Three

It was November. The days were getting colder and shorter. It had been almost two months since I saw Carter in the elevator. I knew when Carter typically arrived and left his office, so I tried hard to not arrive or leave during those times. It made life simpler.

The past two months, I had learned so much about myself. I had to do more things that made 'me' happy. Learning martial arts and art became my passions. I started to take Jujitsu classes on Tuesday and Thursday evenings for self-defense. I figured I should learn how to protect myself. Most of the time, I felt unsafe and looked over my shoulder everywhere I went. It was an eerie feeling, when I walked outside of my office or apartment building. Even after two months, I was scared to be alone or afraid of the shadows lurking around the corner. I was always on guard. There were times, I thought about hiring security staff but felt it was an unnecessary expense. Martial arts had given me confidence to defend myself, if I was involved in a situation once again.

On Saturday afternoons, I attended an art class, at the gallery up the street from my apartment. I enjoyed expressing myself through different arts mediums. It was fun to meet new people and do something other than work. I realized I needed other interests and personal goals.

Eventually, I began to feel like my old self. I was independent and happy. I bought the cutest kitten, from a sphynx breeder. Some people would say she was ugly but I see her beauty. She was a hairless cat. I had always been interested in this breed. She was twelve weeks old and had lived with me for two weeks. She had settled in nicely into my apartment. She had her favorite sleeping spots and loved curling up in her blankets. I named her Lola.

It was a beautiful fall morning. I decided to go for a walk to 'Coffee for the Soul'. It was my new favorite coffee shop. I would go there on weekends, for my morning coffee. I would sit in the comfortable lounge chairs, and read a book or newspaper for an hour. Reading romance novels was my newfound pastime.

"My name is Michael. I own this coffee shop." He held out his hand to shake mine.

"Nice to meet you, I'm Cerise."

"I like to introduce myself to our regulars."

"I guess I've become predictable. I'm here every Saturday morning."

"Very predictable! Medium hazelnut coffee with cream and sugar coming right up," we both laughed.

"Thank you. I'll have to change it up a bit next Saturday, to confuse you." I joked.

"You're welcome. Your special lounge chair is available. Next Saturday I am going to put a 'reserved' sign on the chair, just for you. I know it's your favorite seat in the house," he smiled and winked at me. If I did not know any better, I would have thought he was flirting with me. He was an attractive man, probably ten years older than I was. He had dark hair, blue eyes, and the straightest teeth I had ever seen before.

I sat and read my book. I would catch Michael looking over at me from time-to-time. For the first time in two months, I was enjoying the attention from someone other than Carter.

Chapter Twenty-Four

I was waiting, in my office, for a new client to arrive for our initial meeting to discuss personal investments. I heard the door open in my waiting room. I walked out to greet my client.

"Good morning, may I help you?" I asked the man standing with his back to me.

"Yes, I have an appointment," the man replied. He did not turn around.

"You must be Mr. Russ," I asked.

"Actually, Mr. Russo," he corrected, and turned around and faced me. I was staring into the eyes of the man who killed my mother. He looked the same, only older. More wrinkles and thinning hair. He had a twinkle in his eye, which told me he was excited and his adrenaline was building.

"What are you doing here?" I managed to say. *This cannot be happening! What should I do?* My body was in shock. My palms started to sweat. I heard my heart beat in my ears. A part of me was amazed and confused on why he had not tried anything, in the past two months. I had been vulnerable and alone. My senses told me he watched everything I did for the past two and a half months. I had not been able to go anywhere without looking over my shoulder. I always looked for an alternate street or store to go into for help. I had my routine memorized to prevent or to escape from a situation.

My phone was in my pocket. I started to squeeze my phone, wanting to pull it out and call 911. I felt trapped. *How can I get out of here?* Tony blocked the main entrance. It was not an option. There was an exit door located in my boardroom, which I always kept locked. It was a fire escape exit. It was my best option for getting out. I tried to dial 911 secretly. *I hope I dialed it correctly. Please help me! Please help me!* I kept whispering in my head.

"I have some unfinished business I need to take care of," he muttered. "It looks like you're living it up, on your mommy's money. She told me, she changed the beneficiary to my name. Did you know?"

I shook my head no. *Why would I know that? I was sixteen! I did not even know she had an insurance plan.*

"SHE LIED!" he yelled. "The money was supposed to be mine. I want it back. I deserve it. She would not let me touch you, Cerise. She would not let me have you. If she would have, she would still be alive."

I stood there listening. I was too afraid to move. I did not know what to say or do. I felt faint. I realized I was holding my breath. I opened my mouth and started to breathe to stay calm.

"I'm going to have you, today," he spoke softly. His head was tilted down but looking up at me through his evil eyes.

"Tony, you don't want to do anything you will regret," I pleaded, trying to remain calm. "If you want the money, I will give you the money. I can get you help."

"I don't want your help. I'm perfectly sane. I knew what I was doing, when I killed your mother. I also know, I'm going to fuck you and kill you today, too," he smiled wickedly.

"I'm going to call the police," I threatened.

"Like your friend did, the night I killed your mother? That BITCH," he mumbled. "After I have you, I'm going after her. She ruined my life."

"You ruined your life." I stepped back behind the reception desk and almost tripped on something on the floor. I looked down. It was Jagger. Blood was coming from his head. I screamed in horror. *Why was Jagger even here? I have not seen him for two months. Why is he lying on my floor injured? What is going on?*

"Don't worry, he will live. Your security guards could not stop me from coming here today." He calmly pulled out a gun, and pointed it at me.

"Wait! I thought you wanted the money. If you kill me, how will you get the money?" I started to panic with fear. I was alone. My body trembled uncontrollably. *Was this how, my life was going to end?*

"The money is not any good to me anymore. My life is over. It does not matter," he muttered. He stared at his gun and aimed it directly at my head. I tried to run to the boardroom. He tackled me to the ground. His gun fell and slid across the hardwood floor towards the bathroom. He held my wrist together and started to put his hands on me roughly, rubbing over my breasts with one hand.

I squeezed my eyes closed and yelled, "No!" I was letting my fear paralyze my body. I tried to think about what my sensei taught me in the dojo. I was not going to give in, without a fight. I escaped from his hold and managed to hurt his arm, when I did. I stood up and backed up towards the boardroom. He shuffled over to his gun, picked it up, and pointed it at me.

"I see you are a little stronger than you use to be." He looked at me with his dagger eyes, "I'm up for the challenge." He charged at me again, before he reached me, his gun went off. It was loud. There was a scuffle of someone else in the room. Tony landed on me and I fell back and hit my head on the corner of something hard and sharp. It felt like slow motion. I no longer felt anything. My eyes were blacking out. Someone tackled Tony off me. I slowly turned my head in the direction where two people were fighting. I saw Carter. He had tackled Tony off me. He fought him and tried to keep him away from me. *I was so confused. Why was Carter in my office?* Tony punched Carter in the face and his stomach a few times. It looked like Carter's face was bleeding. Carter was angry, which was not a typically side of his personality. Carter punched Tony in the jaw and knocked him out. Tony was on the floor, unconscious. The room suddenly was silent. Carter rushed to my side.

"Cerise! Cerise! Stay with me," I heard Carter's voice. "Stay with me!" Through my peephole vision, I could see Carter's face leaned over mine. My vision was darker and darker. I could not speak. Tears ran down the sides of my face. Carter leaned in and gave me a kiss on my lips. I could not respond. "Please stay with me!" A tear rolled down his cheek.

Then it was total darkness.

I could not see or feel my body, but I could still hear. I heard Ray barking orders at a few people in the room. He told them to call the police and three ambulances. There were people walking around me. I sensed the panic in the room. I could hear Carter talking to someone on the phone.

"Carter, here. We need you. I do not know if she will make it. She is not responding, but still has a faint heartbeat. Jagger is down and needs medical treatment. Ray is securing the scene." I could only hear Carter's side of the conversation. It sounded like Kyle had many questions, which Carter tried to answer, in his shaken voice. He ended the call and stayed with me.

"Kyle is on his way, Cerise. Hang in there," Carter whispered in my ear.

I was weak. I was confused. *What happened to me? Was I dying? Is Jagger going to be okay? Where was Tony? Why was Carter here?* I started to see memories flash before me. My dad's hugs when he arrived home from work. My Mom's laughter when Daddy and I tickled her. My grandmother's soft voice when she read bedtime stories to me. The first time I met Carter in Art class. The time we walked hand-in-hand on the beach and the night Carter asked me to marry him. They were happy memories of my life.

"Don't leave me," Carter kept on repeating. I heard Kyle arrive along with the paramedics. They moved carefully around me, attached monitors, and assessed my situation. Everyone's voices were muffled, and hard to understand. I could not hear as clearly as before. I was scared, cold, and confused. My senses faded. I felt my body shutting down...

Chapter Twenty-Five

I opened my eyes. The bright sunshine from the window made me squint. Everything was white and sterile. It took me a few minutes to focus and look around the room. I was in a hospital room. It looked like a private room. Carter sat in a chair, pulled up close to my bed. His head rested on the side of my bed and he held my hand. I squeezed my hand slightly. Carter immediately lifted his head to look at me. He smiled gently and then kissed my hand. He looked tired, as if he had not slept for a week.

"Hey, I was wondering when you were going to wake up. How do you feel?"

"My head hurts," I answered. Carter stood up and kissed me on my forehead.

"I will be right back. I have to find a doctor or a nurse."

After he left the room, I looked around to find the room filled with flowers and cards. I noticed a huge teddy bear sitting on a chair in the corner. Carter returned with the doctor two steps behind him.

"I am Dr. Steeles. How are you feeling?" he asked. He was a short man with grey, thinning hair. He pulled my chart off the front of my bed and began making some notes.

"I have a headache."

"The nurse is bringing something for your head in a couple of minutes. Do you mind if I take your blood pressure and temperature." I shook my head in agreement. "Do you recall what happened to you, Miss Brooks?"

"Yes, I remember everything until the paramedics arrived. I don't recall anything afterwards."

"That is good news. You arrived at the hospital unconscious. You have a concussion. You hit your head extremely hard. That is why your head hurts. With some rest, you will be back to normal. We ran tests and there is minimal swelling. You are lucky." Dr. Steeles reported. "We will run a few more tests and if everything is good you are free to go. Probably in a couple of hours with strict rules for home."

"Thank you, Dr. Steeles." He nodded and left the room.

I looked at Carter with so many questions. "I'm so confused. Why are you here? Why did you come to my office? Why was Jagger in my office?"

"Ray and Jagger were on duty. They've been watching you for the past two months to make sure you were safe."

"What? I thought..."

"I know. The truth is I couldn't let you go unprotected with Tony still out there."

"You did not return my calls or texts. After that day in the elevator, I stopped calling you."

"I'm sorry about not returning your calls and how I behaved in the elevator."

"Why did you come to my office?"

"You called me. I was in my office when my phone started to ring. I had not heard from you in two months. I was curious to know why you were calling unexpectedly. When I picked up the phone, I heard your whole conversation with Tony. I immediately rushed downstairs from my office."

"I didn't call you though."

"You must have hit speed dial. Remember I set it up for you a while back?"

"I heard a gun shot. When Tony tackled me, I thought he shot me. I could not feel or see anything. Everything was black. I felt like I was dying. I had visions go through my head of the times I was happy, in my life."

"Yes, it was scary. If only I had arrived moments earlier, I could have prevented it."

"It's not your fault. Will Jagger be okay? I was shocked to see him on the floor."

"Yes, he will be fine."

"Why was he there?" I wondered.

"They have been watching you from a distance. They noticed someone enter the building with Tony's description. They were in the car when they spotted him. Jagger headed to your office while Ray parked the car. When Jagger arrived he was confronted by Tony, who hit him over the head with an object."

"And what about Tony?"

"He passed away shortly after he arrived at the hospital."

"What? How?"

"When I arrived, Tony was charging at you, he fired his gun and landed on top of you. I pushed him off you, to stop the attack. We had had a physical fight. During the fight, I knocked him out. When he regained consciousness, he charged at me with his gun in his hand. My back was facing him. I did not see him charging at me because I was with you. There was a lot of commotion, which resulted in Kyle shooting him."

"I don't remember."

"You were unconscious when it happened. The paramedics were on site looking after you."

"That is crazy."

"Well, I'm happy he can't hurt you anymore." He looked deep into my eyes and kissed my hand. "I really thought I was going to lose you." He leaned over me and gave me a kiss on my lips. It sent chills through my body. He still had that effect on me. I had missed him so much. The past two months have been miserable for me. I cried a lot in the beginning, but I was finally started to live again and do the things I loved.

"Carter, I'm so grateful to you, for everything you did. Who knows where I'd be right now if you didn't show up when you did." I looked into his eyes. "So much time has passed since I spoke to you, and so much has happened. I think you are feeling guilty. You said it was best we move on. You've moved on and I've moved on." I looked at him sadly. "You didn't trust me. You did not want to hear my side. I was hurting too."

"I know, Cerise. I made a mistake. I'm so sorry."

"My world was upside down, and you didn't give me the time of day. I really needed you."

"I know the truth now."

"How?"

"Jagger and Max told me everything after the incident. Three weeks ago, Alec came to see me and admitted everything he had done. Including the day he kissed you." He took my hand and kissed it. "Please forgive me."

"I forgive you but it doesn't change anything. You have moved on. I saw you with that pretty woman. It didn't take long for you to move on to someone else."

The nurse knocked on the door and interrupted us. "Mr. Blake, how is our patient doing?" She was a beautiful Jamaican woman. She was probably in her late forties. I instantly liked her. She was happy and cheerful.

"She seems to be doing well." He stood up and walked over to the door, to give her the extra space on the side of the bed. The nurse started to take my vitals and recorded them in the file. She took some blood for some tests.

"These are for your headache." She handed me a little cup with medicine and water.

"Thank you."

"Mr. Blake has been by your side the entire time. He must be your guardian angel." She bent down close and whispered. "But girl, I have never seen a guardian angel who looked like that before. You must be doing something right," we both smiled. "Now you take care of yourself. You hear." She left the room and winked at Carter. Carter looked sexy as he leaned up against the wall, with his arms crossed. His dress shirt had several buttons undone. He had a cut covered with a butterfly Band-Aid, above his left eye, from where Tony hit him.

Carter returned to his chair to sit beside me. He did not attempt to take my hand again. He knew I was not happy.

"The woman you seen me with was my cousin. She needed a ride to the airport. She was leaving for New York City to meet her husband. He relocated there for business. She stayed behind to sell the house and pack everything. She was excited to be finally moving to New York City to join her husband."

"What? You knew how it looked. You knew it would hurt me. Why would you do that?"

"I know. I did not handle the situation well. I should not have let you assume the worst. The last two months have been extremely difficult for me. A day hasn't gone by that I didn't think of you or wanted to call you." He reached for my hand and caressed it gently. "I've really missed you, Ma Cerise."

"Why didn't you call? What stopped you?"

"I wasn't nice to you, the last time we seen each other. You stopped calling me and I felt that maybe I had ruined my chance to be with you ever again. Ray and Jagger would give me updates on what you were doing the past two months. They told me you seemed happy," Carter explained. "Many Saturday mornings I would go to the coffee shop, you go to each week, to see you. I would wait in my car trying to get up the nerve to go in and talk to you. I was afraid you'd reject me."

"Carter, you're my best friend. I have spent seventeen years of my life with you. I have never been happier with anyone else. You should have talked to me."

"Sorry for the interruption! Can we come in to visit our daughter-in-law to be?" Mrs. Blake asked as she opened the door. *Daughter-In-Law to be?*

"Of course. Please come in," Carter stood up to greet his parents.

"You are looking well. I hope this means you will be on your feet in no time." Mr. Blake said.

"I think I will be released in a couple of hours, if the tests come back fine," I answered.

"Wonderful news." Mrs. Blake kissed my forehead. "My son has been a mess. He would not leave your side. I think this is the first time I have seen him cry since he was an infant." She patted Carter on the shoulder. "Must be true love."

"That it is, Mom." Carter did not take his eyes off me.

It was nice to see Mr. and Mrs. Blake. They spoke to me as if nothing between Carter and I have changed. It was confusing. A short while after, Carter and I were alone in the hospital room, once again.

"Why did she call me daughter-in-law to be?" I looked at him blankly.

"I couldn't tell them! It would have broken their hearts. I had hoped we'd get back together before I'd have to explain anything to them or my brothers," Carter explained. "They were suspicious when I told my mom to hold off on the wedding plans."

"What did she say?"

"She was concerned, but I explained we wanted to have more time to plan the perfect wedding."

"It would have been perfect. It's hard to believe we would have been getting married in less than two weeks."

"You would have made me a happy man. I let my jealousy and insecurity ruin everything. I'm new to this relationship thing." Carter kissed my hand again. "Will you take me back? You are everything to me. Not having you in my life for the last two months has made me realize how much you mean to me. I can't live without you."

I began to cry. I had been waiting so long to hear Carter say this. I had rehearsed each word, repeatedly in my mind of how I would make him regret his choice. I would walk away from him for good because my life was better without him. I was so angry how he did not trust or believe me. I hated the fact; he was not there for me when my biggest opportunity for my career fell through. I was devastated; he started dating a couple of weeks after we broke up. It was my chance to recite every hateful word to perfection.

"Carter, I do not know what to say," I said honestly.

"Please say you'd like to try again. We will take everything slow this time. I promise to never treat you that way again. I will always treat you with respect and always trust you. I want to be there for you."

"Okay," I whispered. I could not say those hateful words that I had rehearsed repeatedly. I wanted him more than ever.

Carter stood up and leaned over the bed to give me a passionate kiss. "I've missed you so much."

Chapter Twenty-Six

"Carter! Are you ready to go?" I yelled down the hallway towards his bedroom. "Phillip is waiting to drive us to the airport." It was unusual for Carter to be running late. He was always punctual and prepared for everything. Our bags were packed. We were ready to go on the Caribbean Cruise; Carter gave me for my birthday. I was excited. I imagined the sand between my toes and the sun's heat on my face. Winter had come early in Toronto. I could not wait to say goodbye to the cold winter temperatures. It was perfect timing for a vacation in the South.

Carter walked down the hallway towards me. He was wearing black Ralph Lauren jeans and a black polo shirt. His dirty blond hair was perfectly finger-combed through. His smile was contagious.

"Are you in a rush?" he teased me. "I love that you are so excited to leave! Before we go, I want to talk to you about something." He guided me over to sit down on the sofa.

He had the rare nervous look on his face. I wondered what bad news was about to pop up. Usually when things are going good for me, something bad always happens. I rubbed my sweaty palms over my jeans.

"These past two weeks have been truly amazing. You have made me the luckiest man alive." He took my hand and place something in it. "I would be honored if you would wear this again."

I looked in my hand. It was my engagement ring. I had left it on Carter's dresser the day I moved out two and half months ago. It sparkled. I looked at Carter with loving eyes. "I would love to." Tears sprung to my eyes.

Carter took the ring out of my hand and placed it on my ring finger. We both knew it was a symbol of our love for each other. One day I would be married to this wonderful man. Our future was ours to explore together.

"I will love you, always and forever." Carter said sincerely.

"I love you too." I entangled my fingers in his and kissed him passionately.

Acknowledgements

A couple of years ago, the story of Cerise and Carter played constantly in my mind. The story developed in my head for a few months, until one day, I sat at my computer and began to write it. Once I started, I became infatuated with writing everyday. It was my little secret hobby and creative outlet.

Once I finished my first draft, I began to think more seriously about having it published. I began to do a lot of research, to educate myself about the publishing world, and I continue to learn new information each day. I have so much respect for writers, editors, and publishers.

I have to acknowledge a few people for my writing journey to this point. Without you, this book would never have been completed.

My Husband: You were the first person to encourage me to write this book. I remember the night I shared my story idea with you…you responded in such a positive and supportive way. I will be forever grateful to you, for your encouragement.

My Children: Although you have not read my book, you have been so supportive in many ways. Thank you for choosing the beautiful cover for *Entangled*; I love it. Love you xoxo

My Sister: You have always been there for me, throughout my entire life. It is only natural for you to be the first person in my family, to read my finished manuscript. Thank you for proofreading my manuscript and giving me your honest feedback.

My Editor: Alethea, you are an amazing editor who gave me wonderful feedback and gentle criticism that made my first book what it is today. I learned so much through my first editing experience because of you. Thank you for everything. I look forward to working with you in the future.

About the Author

Entangled is T.M.Wells' debut novel. Her writing journey began a couple of years ago with a story idea that was always on her mind. She is an entrepreneur and loves to spend her spare time writing, reading, and drawing.

She lives outside of Toronto, Canada with her husband and three children. She grew up in the city but loves nature walks, cottage life, and camping with her family.

CONNECT with T.M.Wells

Website
www.tmwells.com

Facebook
www.facebook.com/tmwellsauthor

Twitter
www.twitter.com/AuthorTMWells

Instagram
www.instagram.com/author.tmwells

Pinterest
www.pinterest.com/authortmwells

Contact/Blog
www.tmwells.com/contact